"This is the first moment I haven't worried about Pops...

"...at least, since we started this trip."

Gus chuckled and shook his head. "Really? Even with the car troubles? And throwing your schedule out the window and having everything up in the air? I'm finding that a little hard to believe."

"This clean air and pretty views are probably doing more for him than anything else I could have done at home," Cecily admitted. "Sounds corny, huh? Besides, I didn't say I wasn't worried about how we're going to get to Lighthouse Bay and whatever else lies ahead of us on this adventure."

"You're seeing it as an adventure now."

"Trying to." She turned to look at him. "And someone told me that I need to enjoy the journey more."

He looked into her eyes. "Sounds like a really wise man."

Then she smiled, and he felt his chest tighten.

He reached up and pushed back a strand of hair that had fallen out of her ponytail...

Dear Reader,

In my life, I have been privileged to help as a caregiver to both my father and stepfather in the last months of their lives. Those were days full of worry and stress, but also joy and peace. When you know the end of someone's life is coming, you sort out what is important from what isn't necessary. You never lose a chance to tell them you love them.

In this book, Cecily Karsten has been entrusted with caring for her grandfather Burt as he faces the end of his life. One of his last wishes is to return to his boyhood home in Michigan's upper peninsula to show her where he came from and say goodbye to the life that made him into the man he has become. Their companion on this road trip is Gus, a neighbor and close friend.

And as often happens on road trips, things don't go as planned, but events turn out as they're supposed to. Detours become opportunities. Love is found and rekindled. And life, above all, is celebrated.

Hold your loved ones close and never miss a chance to tell them you love them.

Syndi

HEARTWARMING

The Teacher's
Unexpected Gift

—

Syndi Powell

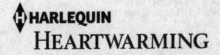

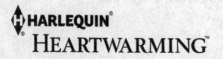

HARLEQUIN®
HEARTWARMING™

ISBN-13: 978-1-335-47561-9

The Teacher's Unexpected Gift

Copyright © 2023 by Cynthia Powell

For questions and comments about the quality of this book, please contact us at CustomerService@Harlequin.com.

Harlequin Enterprises ULC
22 Adelaide St. West, 41st Floor
Toronto, Ontario M5H 4E3, Canada
www.Harlequin.com

Printed in U.S.A.

Recycling programs for this product may not exist in your area.

Syndi Powell started writing stories when she was young and has made it a lifelong pursuit. She's been reading Harlequin romance novels since she was in her teens and is thrilled to be on the Harlequin team. She loves to connect with readers on her Facebook author page, Facebook.com/syndipowellauthor.

Books by Syndi Powell

Harlequin Heartwarming

When Love Comes Calling
Soldier of Her Heart
Their Forever Home

Matchmaker at Work

A Merry Christmas Date
The Bad Boy's Redemption
A Hero for the Holidays

Hope Center Stories

Finding Her Family
Healing Hearts
Afraid to Lose Her

Visit the Author Profile page
at Harlequin.com for more titles.

This book is dedicated to some of my favorite teachers: Mr. Hooks, Mr. Cosart, Mr. Madorski, Mr. Bassett and Mlle McClelland. The impact you had on my life and those of your students could never be measured because you cared about us and taught from your passion to educate and grow young minds.

CHAPTER ONE

CECILY SIGNED THE divorce paperwork with the last name she'd chosen to take back since her husband—correction, ex-husband—had decided that she wasn't worthy of claiming his any longer. Cecily Karsten once again after a little more than a decade of marriage that she had thought had been wonderful. Where had it gone wrong? She was still trying to figure that out. She looked up at the clerk who then passed the paperwork to Tom for his signature.

"Is that it?" Cec asked. "Is it over?"

The clerk nodded and stamped the pages with an official-looking seal. "I'll make you both copies, then you're free to go." She left them standing at the counter, and Cec turned to glance at Tom. He was wearing a suit and tie, just like he usually did when they'd been married. As if the day was another ordinary one, and not life changing.

She quickly looked away. It had now become painful to gaze at his familiar features and wonder when they would become fuzzy in her memory. Would it take six months to get over him? A year? Or would she be longing for something she couldn't have for a lifetime?

"After she gives us our copies, did you want to go get a drink or something? Maybe a late lunch?" Tom asked from behind her.

Cec turned back to stare at him. Was that some kind of sick joke? He'd told her on Christmas Day that he didn't want to be married anymore, and could she kindly find somewhere else to live by New Year's. And now he wanted to get a drink with her?

She felt her jaw tighten and her eyes narrow, her pain turning into anger. Tom held up his hands. "Okay, okay. It was just an idea. Forget I said anything."

Obviously, it had been a bad idea. The worst one he might have ever had. Except for the one where he kicked her out of his life and his home. She tapped her fingernails on the counter as they continued to wait. Finally, the clerk returned with warm copies of their divorce decree in hand. Cec took them and started to flee from the court building, pausing only for the elevator that would deliver her to the parking garage below. She heard Tom's clopping footsteps nearing, and she reached over to press the down button several times, wishing the elevator would arrive sooner. The doors opened, and she rushed inside and repeatedly pressed the sublevel two button until the elevator doors shut a moment after Tom stepped inside.

"Couldn't you have waited for the next elevator?" she said, her voice tinged with anger.

He glanced at her, then at the lit display as the floor numbers descended. "Why would I wait when this one was available?"

"Maybe because I don't want to spend another minute with you."

"Real mature, Cecily. I had hoped we could at least be civil with each other."

She bit back the urge to stick her tongue out at him since it would only prove his point. "I am civil." Barely. Though she usually tried to be polite at the least.

He snorted as if he didn't believe her, but she didn't really care. Nothing he thought concerned her anymore. She took a deep breath at that thought. Once, he'd been her whole life. Her reason for breathing. He'd consumed her thoughts and dreams and moments. She closed her eyes and pressed a hand to her forehead.

"What are your plans now that school is out for the summer?" Tom asked.

She reached over and pressed the sublevel two button again. They must have taken the world's slowest elevator since time seemed to be moving backward. She glanced up at the lit floor display. Were they even moving?

The elevator stopped, the doors opened, but it wasn't the right floor. She considered getting off and waiting for the next elevator, but a group of people stepped forward, and she had to move to the back to give them space. Unfortunately, this moved Tom closer to her as well. She rolled her eyes. "I don't have my summer planned yet."

"Really? You usually have an agenda for every minute until it's time to return to school. What's different this year?"

She glanced at him. Had he really asked that? Instead of verbally answering, she gave a noncommittal shrug and sighed in relief as the elevator doors opened to reveal the parking garage. She walked off the elevator and headed toward her car, keys in hand and steps brisk and unfaltering. She couldn't wait to change out of these heels. She had chosen to dress up for her divorce proceedings in part to show Tom what he would be missing. But as she walked through the garage, her toes pinched and arches aching, she would have traded them for her comfortable ballerina flats without hesitation.

She reached her car and pressed the button on her key fob to unlock the doors. Tom called her name, and she turned in his direction, more out of habit than any desire to see or speak to him again. He held up one finger to make her wait for him. She tapped one foot on the cement floor, the tapping echoing in the cavernous lot.

"Cecily, I just want to say…"

She waited for a moment, wondering what he could possibly offer her now. Apologies for breaking her heart? For upending her life? For making her feel worthless and unloved and full of insecurities?

When he didn't continue, she asked, "What do you want, Tom?"

He glanced down at his shoes then back up at her, a gesture she'd come to know that meant he was sorry. "I only want you to be happy again."

"I was happy. But obviously you weren't." She got inside her car then slammed the door shut on him. She started the engine and paused only to let Tom get out of her way before backing out of the parking space and racing away from this horrible, horrible day.

Once on the street, she turned the volume of the car stereo louder so that it blasted a song that she'd been playing on repeat since Christmas. Her best friend, Vivi, called the tune her comeback song. Cec preferred to think of it as her takeback song because she was going to take back her life from the mess that Tom had left it in. Take back her freedom and her independence. Take back her confidence and purpose. She smiled and turned the volume up one more notch.

The computer display on her car's dashboard lit up, informing her that she had an incoming call on her cell phone. She smiled at the name before pressing the button to answer. "Hey, Vivi."

"Hey, yourself. How did it go?"

Cec hesitated, reflecting on the events of the morning. "Well, I'm not lying in a crumpled, crying mess on the floor of my car, so I'd say that it went better than I expected."

Vivi made a noise on the other end of the phone. "Girl, please. You've got more strength in you than to allow that jerk to get to you."

Cec bit her lip as she thought about Tom's request for a drink and her refusal. "I might have been a bit prickly with him today."

"Like he didn't deserve that."

"Well, I could have been nicer. But when he asked me to get a drink with him after…"

"He did what?"

"Why would he ask me that? Today of all days? We had just signed the paperwork to dissolve our marriage, for goodness' sake. There was no way I wanted to spend another five minutes rehashing what happened."

"Well…"

Cec slowed the car as it approached a red light. "You think I should have agreed to go?"

"I'm not saying you should have gone, but maybe you would have gotten some answers out of him."

"Answers?"

"Like why he suddenly wanted out. Why did he tell you at Christmas? And was he really seeing someone on the side?"

"I told you I was only wondering about that. Not that he really was."

"Okay, but you might have gotten…"

"What? Closure?" She started to accelerate when the light turned green. "Maybe I could have. But it's too raw right now. I just signed the papers. I need more time before I'm willing to pick at that scab."

"Okay, okay, fair enough." Vivi paused on the other end. "Do you want to get together tonight? I'm in the middle of grading final papers, but we could grab some dinner."

"I thought you and Brian had a charity thing to go to."

"I can cancel. He'll understand that you

need me more because you're my best friend and you're hurting."

"I'm not hurting." She said the words then realized they were true. She'd had almost six months to come to terms with this change in her life. She might be a little bitter right now. Okay, a lot bitter, but it was getting better. And she didn't cry herself to sleep every night like she had at the beginning. She had come to accept this monumental change in her life. "Go out with your boyfriend. I'm fine. Besides, I've got Pops."

"We'll plan a night out together soon though. I heard they're doing a trivia night, at the pub next Friday."

Cec laughed. "Jasper has been talking about wanting a rematch since we creamed him and his team the last time." Jasper had an ongoing rivalry with Cec and Viv ever since they'd beaten his team at the pub's trivia night three years ago. It only fueled the fun on those evenings.

"We needed to get him back for his team beating us before that. We can't allow him to win ever again. I can't handle the humiliation."

"You and your competitive side."

"Love you, girl. Call me later if you want to talk."

Arriving back at her grandfather's house, a tan brick bungalow, Cec lowered the music volume before turning off the car. She'd moved in with Pops this past winter when he'd been diagnosed with terminal cancer and wasn't sure how long he'd have.

She stepped out of the car and looked down the oak tree–lined street. She could hear shouts from kids, who, now free on summer vacation, rode their bikes up and down the neighborhood at any time. Glenda from across the street called a greeting. Cec held up a hand in response, then slammed the car door shut.

She entered the code for the garage door which rose before she ducked under it and walked up to the door to the house. Pops would be inside waiting to hear all the gory details of her divorce proceedings. And to be honest, the moment wasn't something she wanted to relive just yet. But there was no reason to stay in the garage when he had probably heard her arrive.

She took the back door into the house

and pressed the garage door button to close it behind her. Entering from the kitchen, she could hear voices coming from the living room, hushed below the hiss of her grandfather's oxygen machine, a squat thing he'd nicknamed Faulkner. Early on when he'd been put on oxygen, he'd chosen nicknames for each of the machines, reflecting Pops's love for American literature. There was Faulkner, the tall, thin one was Hemingway and the backpack air condenser was called Twain.

She placed her purse on the kitchen counter then happily kicked off her heels before leaning over to pick them up with two fingers. She started to walk toward the living room where she could tell from the voices that her grandfather's neighbor Gus was sitting with him. Even though his name sounded like it belonged to a man her grandfather's age, Gus was mid-thirties, like her. And hot. He could melt ice just by looking at it with that brown-eyed smolder of his. But what was he doing here in the middle of the day during the week? Didn't the man ever work? Seemed like he was here at all times of the day.

The two of them had built a friendship when Gus had moved in next door during the weekend of the annual Army-Navy football game. Pops had gone over to introduce himself, heard the game playing on the radio and had declared that Navy would beat Army, having joined the Navy right after high school. Gus had been an Army medic, so he bet Pops that Army would win, wagering that the loser would have to shovel the winner's driveway and sidewalks all winter. Pops had won that bet but had allowed Gus to use his snow blower every snowfall. Their friendship had only deepened over the last eighteen months.

"The thing is if we're going to do this, we need to do it quick. The sooner, the better," Gus was saying.

Cec stopped at the doorway, retreating a little so that she wouldn't be seen. Those two were obviously up to something.

"I agree with you, son. I just don't know how to tell her. She's not going to like it." That was her grandfather's voice. He sounded a bit worried. What in the world were they planning?

"This is your life, not hers. And if this

is what you want, then she'll just have to understand. Doesn't matter if she likes it or not."

Pops sighed. "You're right. Time is running out."

Cec took a deep breath and released it. She knew he wasn't going to get better. In fact, she'd watched him slowly decline over the last few months. The doctors didn't offer much hope at this point. Whatever time her grandfather had left, she would make sure he would be comfortable. That's all she had left to give him.

"Then we need to do this now. Before it's too late."

"Okay. I've got a doctor's appointment next week that I have to be at, but we can hit the road after. Sound good?"

Cec stepped into the living room to glare at the two men sitting close to each other in the recliners. "I don't know what the two of you are planning, but no one is going anywhere."

Gus stared at Cecily, who stood, hands on her hips, looking as if she would spit nails if she could. Burt loved his granddaughter, but Gus was less convinced that she was as great a person as he claimed. Uptight, sure. Bitter, but for a good reason with the recent divorce. Beautiful, definitely. Though the scowl on her face didn't enhance her high cheekbones, it did light a fire to her baby blue eyes. But she was no saint, despite Burt's insistence.

Burt turned to his granddaughter. "How long have you been home?"

"Long enough to hear that you're scheming something. A road trip?" She walked farther into the room to loom over her grandfather's recliner. "Tell me that I heard wrong because there is no way you're traveling any distance away from here."

Burt held up his hand, quick to explain. "You didn't hear wrong. I don't want to spend my last days on earth cooped up in this house. I want to get out and see things."

"What about your oxygen machine? What about all your appointments? And your prescriptions?" She shook her head vigorously, but it didn't even make her blond hair fall out of her tight bun. "You are not, I repeat not. Going. Anywhere."

Gus held up his hands to indicate a time

out. "Now wait a minute, Cecily. Why don't you hear him out before you shoot this down?"

She then focused those steely blue eyes on Gus. "I knew you would be behind this harebrained plan. You can break all the rules you want to with your life, but you leave my sick grandfather out of this."

He mirrored her stance, putting his hands on his hips. "You don't even know what we've got in mind."

"I don't need to know. I've heard all I care to." Cecily crouched down beside her grandfather. "Pops, listen to reason, please. This is not the time to be traipsing around town or anywhere for that matter."

"Gus is right."

Cecily's head shot back as if he'd stunned her. "He's what?"

She scowled at Gus, but even her anger couldn't dim the smile on his face. To further annoy her, he gave her a wink. "Ha! He said I was right."

"I heard what he said," she managed to say through gritted teeth. She turned back to her grandfather. "I know you've been depressed lately…" Burt waved a hand in her direction, but she continued to talk. "But this is the time we should be preparing for the inevitable."

"That's what I am doing, baby girl. Ticking items off my bucket list." Burt reached over and put a hand gently on her head. "Doing things one last time before I die."

Cecily stiffened at the last word. Burt had told Gus she had trouble saying the *d* word. She would talk about the inevitable or the end or anything else, but the word *death* would not pass her lips. He'd seen it a lot on the job, with families of terminal patients who were finding it hard to accept the truth about their loved ones. He'd transported enough patients who still tried to do what they used to and ended up falling and hurting themselves. He'd often sat in the back of the ambulance and held hands with someone who was afraid of what the end could be.

Gus rose to his feet. "We're only talking one day. Not a week or a month. And not even a full day. More like an afternoon."

Burt touched his granddaughter's cheek. "I want to go one last time to Little Bavaria. Eat some chicken and noodles. Listen to an oompah band. And maybe reminisce about the last time I took your granny there for her birthday. That doesn't seem so horrible, does it?"

Cecily sighed and shook her head. "No, it sounds wonderful. But I'm just worried about you."

"I know."

Gus watched the moment between grandfather and granddaughter, and an ache formed in the middle of his chest. His granddad had passed away just after he got discharged from the army almost a decade ago. The time Gus had lost with him left a bitter taste in his mouth. He'd do anything to go back to those days. Maybe that's why he cherished his friendship with Burt. Because in some ways, he was like Granddad. A crotchety old man, Burt liked to call himself, but truth was he was a good man. Sincere. Humble. And Burt always had time to give him advice, and he needed a lot of it.

The fact that their time together grew short only made these moments sweeter.

And made the time that was left more urgent.

Gus cleared his throat. "We could go on

a day that has cooler weather and during the week so the town will be less crowded."

Cecily rose to her full height, which he guessed was all of five foot five inches if she wore heels, yet her demeanor made him feel smaller, and he was well over six feet tall. She gave him a scolding look that reminded him of a strict calculus teacher he'd once had. All she needed to complete the ensemble would be to wear glasses that sat on the edge of her nose. "It doesn't matter what day it is or what the weather is like. My grandfather is not going." Burt started to protest, and Cecily put a hand on his shoulder and continued. "At least, you're not going without me."

Gus wanted to roll his eyes at this pronouncement. "What? Your mere presence will stop any harm from happening?"

"No, but at least I'll be there if something does happen to his health or well-being."

Gus came to stand next to her and folded his arms over his chest. "I have superior medical training, so we don't need you."

She glared at him and put her fists on her hips again. "Well, I am his medical proxy and have to give consent for any treatment he might receive, so you *will* take me along."

It was a good old-fashioned stand-off. They glowered at each other silently for several minutes. Gus swore that her left eye twitched, but she didn't blink. And he wasn't going to be the first one to do so. He concentrated on the dark blue circles around the baby blue irises of her eyes. Although her eyes looked less sky blue and more like cloudy gray skies at the moment.

"Okay, folks, I say the three of us all go together." They both turned to face Burt, who gave them a big smile. "Great idea going during the week, especially now that school is out for the summer. We'll choose a day that's not too hot or too busy. I'll even concede to using that horrible wheelchair if I have to, and Gus can push me around Little Bavaria. Good thing it's little." He nodded. "Yep, I'd say this is one of my better ideas. Wouldn't you both agree?"

He smiled at them as if he'd won. Maybe he had.

CHAPTER TWO

CEC CHECKED THE trunk of her car to make sure she had packed two extra tanks of oxygen along with the one that was on the rolling stand Pops would have with him. She'd also included the small tank that looked like a backpack that he would use while they were in the car, although its battery life was shorter. Luckily, she'd bought a converter to fit into the USB port to keep the battery charged as long as the car was running.

She checked the tanks again to make sure their readouts showed them as full. The worst thing would be for them to run out while they were over eighty miles from home. She paused. Maybe this road trip was a bad idea after all. It would be safer for them to stay put. She could look up copycat recipes of Little Bavaria's famous chicken and make it for Burt right here. She gave a decisive nod. She'd simply have to tell him it was too risky and cancel their afternoon trip.

And by doing so, she'd be taking away a little piece of his joy.

But what was more important? Living longer or feeling happy? She'd put all her money into giving him another day, even another hour.

She started to take the first oxygen tank out of the trunk when Pops called her name from where he stood on the front porch, watching her. "You're supposed to be putting them in the car, not taking them out."

She shielded her eyes from the sun that seemed to scorch her. So much for it being cooler weather that day. She walked over to him and stood at the bottom of the porch. "I'm not so sure about this trip anymore."

"What's not to be sure about? It's a few hours."

"A couple hours to drive there. Then a couple hours in Little Bavaria. And a couple more to drive home. That's at least six hours. More than a few."

"Trust a math teacher to keep track of the numbers." Pops took the first step off the porch. He faltered a little, and she reached up to steady him and help him down one stair. "It's going to be fine, baby girl. Just fine."

"You can't know that."

"But I do." He lifted his head toward the sky and closed his eyes as the sun beat down on them. "It's a beautiful sunny day. And I'm ready to blow this popsicle stand and see a little more of the world than the four walls of the house."

"But what if something happens?"

"Then we'll deal with it." He opened his eyes and gestured at the car. "Something tells me you've prepared for any emergency. Extra oxygen tanks. Medical supplies. Even a cooler with a few snacks in case we get hungry on the road."

Her grandfather knew her so well. But then he'd stepped in, along with Granny, to help her mom raise her after her father, their only child, died when she was only eight. "I still think maybe we should postpone the trip. I heard you coughing last night. You could have a buildup of fluid in your lungs that could develop into something worse."

"I cough every night. It's part of the cancer."

"Cancer sucks."

He put a hand on her shoulder as he took the last step to stand on the sidewalk. "Yes, it does. And today is about taking back some of what it's taken away from me."

He lifted his hand to wave a greeting to Gus, who walked over with a large duffel bag. "More medical supplies? What do you two think could possibly happen?" He grimaced.

Gus helped him walk to her car and get settled into the passenger seat. He placed the cannula in Pop's nose and turned on the backpack oxygen machine. "There's nothing wrong with being prepared."

Gus shut the car door then turned to look at Cecily. She glanced at the duffel bag and raised one eyebrow. Gus gave a shrug. "I don't think we're going to need it, but it wouldn't hurt."

"I already packed everything we might need."

"Then we'll be doubly prepared, won't we?" He followed her to the back of the car and placed the oxygen tank she'd taken out back into the trunk and added the duffel bag inside before closing it. "You're sure you don't want me to drive?"

"Positive." She didn't want to give up any control of this day, so that meant she would drive them there and home.

"We might be more comfortable in my SUV than in your car. More legroom at least."

She bristled at his words. Was he really trying to take over this trip? "I think we'll be fine in mine."

Gus shrugged then walked to the rear passenger door and got inside the car. Cecily watched him say something to Pops then laugh. She took a deep breath and reminded herself that this journey was for Pops.

THE SCENERY SEEMED to stagger by the side window. Gus glanced up front to look at the speedometer to see how slowly Cecily drove. "You know the speed limit here is seventy, not fifty, right?"

Cec's eyebrows slammed together, and the muscles of her jaw twitched at his words. For some reason, it tickled Gus that he could affect her like that.

Pops glanced over the seat to peer at him. "My Gladys taught Cecily how to drive when she was fifteen, since Cec's mom was working extra shifts at the hospital that summer. And Gladys, God bless her, never could be accused of having a lead foot."

"Granny taught me everything she knew, and she was a cautious and careful driver."

Pops nodded at Cec. "That she was. And definitely not a speeder."

"We're not in a hurry to get there, so I don't see why the speed I'm driving is any concern." She glanced at Pops then in the rearview mirror at Gus. "To either of you."

Gus gave her a wink, and the muscles in her jaw twitched again. She returned her eyes to the road as he chuckled and sat back in the seat. "You're right. There's no rush." Thank goodness, he thought.

"Did I ever tell you the story of how I met Cecily's grandmother?" Pops didn't wait for an answer but started the story. "I had finished my service in the Navy and was attending Central Michigan's teacher college on the GI bill. One of my professors invited the students over for dinner one Sunday."

"And his daughter Gladys was the one cooking dinner."

Pops turned to Cecily. "Now who's telling the story? You or me?" He shifted toward Gus. "But yes, I took one bite of Gladys's pot roast and fell in love right then and there. Of course, it took three more years for me to convince her to marry me, but it was all worth it in the end."

"Three years?" Gus winced. "I married my second wife a month after our first date."

"Some things are worth waiting for. And my Gladys was surely that."

"Granny wanted to finish her own teaching degree before getting married. It was important to her that she complete what she'd started, and she didn't want being married to stop her from achieving her goal." Cec sighed then glanced at Burt. "She was one amazing woman."

"She was that." Burt reached over and put a hand on Cecily's shoulder. "And I think I miss her more now than I ever have."

Gus knew that Burt's wife had died from cancer, but Burt had been closemouthed about the details. "How long has she been gone?"

Burt cast an eye at Cecily. "It'll be five years this November, right?"

Cec nodded at this, and her grip on the steering wheel tightened. "November eleventh. Stupid cancer."

The mood in the car seemed to darken as they each got quiet. Gus almost regretted asking the question. To get the conversation back on track, he asked, "What did she teach?"

"Science. Physics was her first love. In a different time, she might have focused on research, but she loved teaching high school kids to enjoy science." Pops sighed. "Me, I never saw the fascination for it and preferred literature myself. But I'm happy she got to do what she loved."

"Did the two of you both teach at Thora High?"

"Yep. And now Cecily has taken up the baton we passed to her when we retired and is one of their shining stars."

"Pops." Cecily's cheeks stained a pretty shade of pink.

"What? You almost had that Teacher of

the Year award this past year and the year before."

"Vivi deserved the win this year. Her community project with her senior history class was inspired. She had them interview senior citizens about their lives, and the book based on those conversations will come out next month for the library fundraiser." She sat a little straighter. "But that doesn't mean I won't aim to get it this coming school year."

"That's my girl." Burt gave a bark of laughter, which led to a coughing spell. He waved off Gus's offer of a tissue. "I'm fine. I'm fine."

Cec took a quick look at him before slowing the car down as they approached a turn off from the highway. "Maybe we could use a break."

"It's only been a little over an hour. I'm fine."

She glanced in the rearview mirror at Gus, who gave her a shrug. "He says he's fine. Let's keep going."

She gave a short nod and seemed to press her foot a little more on the accelerator. "I figure we'll be there in about an hour or so. Just in time for lunch."

"Why don't we go to the Christmas store first?" Burt asked. "Work up an appetite before we indulge."

"Pops, I don't know if that's a good idea. What if you get worn out before we even get to the restaurant?"

"Gus is the one who's going to be pushing the wheelchair, so he's more likely to get tired before I do. Please, baby girl. It's been a long time since we've gone there."

Again, those baby blue eyes sought his from the rearview mirror. Shopping didn't sound like a great choice to him, but this was Burt's last-chance trip and he should have some say in how they spent their time. "Why not? It might be fun."

Cecily shook her head. "You have no idea what you just agreed to."

"It's a store. What could be so bad about it?"

An hour later, he stared at the massive shop that could have easily covered five or six football fields, chock full of ornaments, garland, tree skirts, stockings and other Christmas stuff. So much stuff. He could feel his eyes bulging out at the sheer volume of it all. And they played Christmas carols over the speakers. In the middle of June.

"What is this place?" he asked.

"The world's largest Christmas store," Burt answered from the wheelchair. "And we're not going to see much of it if you keep standing here instead of pushing me around like you promised."

Gus grabbed the handles of the wheelchair, and they began their trek around the aisles. Cec spotted something and darted off to a display. She held up an ornament that appeared to be a taco.

"That's a Christmas decoration?"

Cec nodded. "My mom will love it. She'd eat tacos every day if she could." She glanced around then grabbed a red plastic basket from a stack and placed the ornament inside. "She once ate tacos at every meal, including breakfast. Her love for tacos is as real as mine is for equations."

Gus made a face at her. "What's there to love about equations?"

"There's a beautiful mystery waiting to be solved in each one."

"And you like to figure them out?"

"Yes, I do."

She gave him a full smile then, and his breath got caught in his throat. When she smiled like that, it made her shine. And he wanted to be a part of that. He coughed to disguise his attraction before pushing the wheelchair as she darted off to another display.

"My granddaughter is a beautiful woman, wouldn't you say, Gus?"

She made a T-shirt and shorts look as glamorous as an evening gown. He dragged his gaze away from Cecily and looked down at Gus. "You wouldn't be trying to do some matchmaking, would you? Because you know my awful track record with women."

Burt waved his hand. "You just haven't met the right woman yet. Hadn't met my Cecily. She would be a challenge for you, that's for sure."

A challenge? Maybe to his temper. Gus dismissed the idea. "She's not my type. Too serious. Give me a woman who makes me laugh, and now you've got my interest."

"Cecily could make you laugh. And you couldn't do better than her, that's the truth."

"Burt..."

"All right. All right." He held up his hands. "I won't interfere. But I think you should give it a chance. She might surprise you if you actually got to know her."

They pulled up beside where Cecily was looking at more ornaments. Instead of a food theme, these portrayed snowmen dressed for different occupations. She found a teacher and another in a business suit. "For Vivi and Brian."

"They're still together?" Burt asked.

"And going strong despite Vivi's reservations at first." She turned to Gus. "She was convinced she couldn't meet the perfect guy this year because it's cursed. She seems to have one year of bad luck every seven years, so of course this is when she would fall for the love of her life."

He raised an eyebrow at this. "And how is that going?"

"They've had their share of bad luck, but what counts is that they're facing it together. Love wins in the end and all. I think

I'll get them these." She put the ornaments in her basket.

Gus's face must have shown his skepticism because Cecily frowned at him. "What? You don't believe that love conquers all?"

"I believe that hard work can, but love?" He gave a shrug. "Not in my experience."

"So, you're a cynic."

Burt cleared his throat. "Can we go to the bird section? There's something I've been meaning to look at."

Cecily checked the brochure that held a map of the store. With a place this big, they needed it despite the signs that hung from the ceiling indicating the theme of each section. She pointed out the direction they needed to go and led the way there.

"Why birds, Pops? I never knew you were interested in them."

"One bird, in particular." But he didn't elaborate until they pulled in front of a twelve-foot tree covered in every type of bird imaginable. Burt searched the boughs of the pine then pointed at a bright red bird. "That one."

Gus reached up and pulled the ornament

from the tree and handed it to Burt. "Why the cardinal?"

"Legend says that when you see a cardinal, it's the soul of a loved one coming to visit you." Burt rubbed a finger over the bird's metal head. "A few weeks after my Gladys died, I was standing at the kitchen sink staring out the window. I was missing her something horrible and feeling sorry for myself. Suddenly, a cardinal flew by and took a perch on a branch of the tree in the backyard. Stared right in at me. I couldn't look away. I put a hand on the window, and I swear it nodded at me before flying off. I believe Gladys was telling me to stop wallowing in grief and to get on with my life."

Cec kneeled down beside the wheelchair and rested her hand on Burt's. "I never heard that story before."

Burt handed her the cardinal ornament. "I want to buy you this so when you look at it, it will remind you that I'm always watching over you even when I'm gone."

"Pops…"

"Please."

She kept her eyes on her grandfather's

for a moment, then nodded and placed a kiss on his cheek. When she straightened, Gus could see unshed tears glistening in her eyes. She glanced away for a moment, then her eyes landed back on them both.

Gus put a hand on Burt's shoulder. "I don't know about the two of you, but I'm starving. What do you say we buy these and go get some lunch?"

POPS SEEMED TO relish the chicken as he helped himself to a second piece from the platter then spoke to Gus, who ate with as much gusto. "Didn't I tell you? Best chicken in the world."

Cec picked at the chicken leg on her plate. After she nearly broke down in the Christmas store, the last thing she'd wanted was food. But this was Pops's afternoon, and she wouldn't let her tears dim any of his enjoyment. She surveyed the bowls of noodles, buttered vegetables and chicken dressing that covered their groaning table, along with a large boat of gravy, a basket of rolls and a dish of cranberry relish. "My favorite is the spaetzle. I remember Granny tried to make this from scratch once. It turned out okay."

"She tried, bless her. But it couldn't hold a candle to my Oma's." Pops put his elbows on the table and leaned in. "My grandmother was the best cook in the whole world. And the closest I've come to her cooking is here in Little Bavaria."

"Is that why you and your wife came here to celebrate your birthdays?"

Pops nodded and wiped his mouth with the cloth napkin. "Every year like clockwork. But when my Gladys died, well… It didn't feel right to be here without her."

Cec reached over and grabbed his hand. "I'm glad I could come here with you now."

"Me too."

Their server appeared and filled their drink glasses. Pops held up the empty chicken platter. "Could we get another order of chicken to take home?"

The young woman nodded and took the platter with her as she left to enter their takeout order. "More chicken, Pops? You aren't getting enough already?"

"Wouldn't hurt to have a couple pieces to eat on our journey home, would it?"

Gus had cleaned his plate. "I agree. All that walking in the store made me hungry.

And if we're going to explore the town a little more before we leave, why not?"

Cec said, "I guess it's a good thing I brought the cooler with us."

"Just think. We can eat the leftovers for dinner tonight and lunch tomorrow, and you won't have to worry about cooking." Pops reached over and took another helping of dressing. "If only we could eat like this every day."

It felt good to see him eating so much. It seemed like he hadn't had much of an appetite lately, which had worried her. She'd brought it up at the appointment a couple days ago with his doctor, but she had suggested it was normal to see a loss of appetite considering some of the medication that Pops was on. "The neighbors seem to keep us stocked with plenty of meals and baked goods. They're very thoughtful."

Pops agreed. "I sure wouldn't mind if Trudy made more of those cinnamon rolls. They were really good." He turned to Gus. "Did she bring you some of those when you moved in?"

"I don't think so."

"Well, the next time she drops off a batch, I'll try to save you one or two."

The oompah band took their seats on the stage at one end of the restaurant and began to play. Pops paused in his eating to direct his attention toward the stage, closing his eyes. Cec watched him and felt the sting of tears again threatening. She wiped away any evidence of her sorrow before Pops turned back and smiled at the two of them. "This has been a great day, hasn't it?"

Gus glanced at her before nodding. "One of your best ideas."

After the first song, the bandleader approached the microphone. "As part of our annual Summerfest celebration, we like to promote German culture to our tourists. So, before we begin the next song, I'd like to invite any couples who would like to learn a few traditional German dance moves to come up to the space here in front of the stage."

Pops turned to her. "You should go up there."

She put a hand on her chest. "You know my luck with dancing."

"Because you've never found the right

partner." He nudged Gus in the side. "You'll go up there with her, won't you?"

Gus made noises of protest until Pops rapped his fist on the table. "If I could, I'd join on in. But since I can't, you two have to go in my place. This is my day, after all."

That wasn't fair. Nothing like guilt to make her get to her feet and say, "He's right. Let's go."

Gus seemed wary but rose from his chair. She followed him making his way between tables, silently cursing Pops and Gus both for putting her in this position. She didn't want to dance with Gus. Especially with her emotions all over the place today.

At the edge of the stage, Gus faced her. "The old man is good at using guilt to get what he wants."

"True. But he doesn't ask for much. And it will make him really happy." She looked over to find Pops beaming at them.

Gus's gaze followed hers, and he nodded. "I know. Truth is, I'm a little embarrassed. I don't dance in public. Actually, I don't dance at all. I must have been born with two right feet."

"Don't you mean left feet?"

Gus grinned at her. "See? I dance so bad that I can't even get the phrase correct?"

Cec returned his smile as the bandleader walked off the stage and joined the group of six couples, showing them a few moves. Some of the choreography looked too complicated for learning in less than five minutes, but Cec figured she could handle the easier parts. Mainly the steps where the women twirled while the men hopped in the center and clapped hands in time to the music, and the ending, when the couples danced in each other's arms in a large, wide circle.

One of the servers brought out a cardboard box, then gave each woman an apron to tie on over their clothes, and the men each received a hat with a feather.

Gus tied the strings of the apron behind Cecily's back as she glanced at the other volunteers for the dance. "At least I won't be the only one feeling a little ridiculous."

He turned her around and gave her a wink before putting the hat on top of his head. The man seemed to have a problem with looking at her and not giving her a wink, which usually annoyed her. But with the playful mood now between them, it amused her instead.

The music began, and Cec glanced at the server, who started the women off twirling while the bandleader led the men in their hopping and clapping in the center. Cec turned to the left when she should have turned to the right and almost bumped into the woman next to her. She tried to apologize but they were laughing and turning and twirling and then she found herself in Gus's arms, looking up into his smiling face.

She couldn't help but mirror that smile. He might be annoying, but his concern for Pops and wanting to cheer the old man by doing something they were hopelessly bad at revealed he had a good heart. Warmth spread from where she and Gus touched, until it reached her cheeks and had more to do with her attractive dance partner than the physical exertion of the dance itself.

Then the song was over, and Gus removed his arms from her waist. She almost missed them.

When they returned to the table, Pops

smiled and clapped. "That was wonderful. Wonderful. You looked so good out there."

"I almost ran into a woman on one of the turns."

"And I almost fell over when I had to rest my ankle on my knee before hopping on to my other foot." Gus chuckled as he took his seat at the table. "But it was a lot of fun."

"You should go up there and do it again."

Both Cecily and Gus quickly held up their hands and disagreed.

AFTER THEY FINISHED eating, Cecily packaged the leftovers and stored them in the cooler in the trunk of her car. Gus looked up and down the main street of Little Bavaria. Folks had taken the old world German theme to heart in the design of the buildings. Whether the storefronts sold coffee or linens or hardware, the exposed wood frame trim gave them a harmonized look.

Gus turned to find Burt watching him. "I've been living in this state over four years, and I've never visited this place. It's great."

"I'm glad you like it. Perhaps you can

bring my granddaughter here yourself after I'm gone. Treat yourselves on your birthdays like Gladys and I used to, maybe."

"Burt..."

The old man tittered. "I know what you said, but she's a great girl."

Gus spotted Cecily walking towards them. She was more than just a great girl. She was a fine woman who wasn't as uptight as he'd first assumed. Instead, she had a real warmth about her. The fact that she had been willing to embarrass herself in order to entertain Burt showed that she would do anything for the sake of the old man's well-being.

And the fact that she was beautiful didn't hurt.

Cecily smiled at them both. "Who's ready for some shopping?"

The two men groaned but followed her into the first shop. They meandered the long aisles of a country general store that sold everything from penny candies to crystal to sweatshirts advertising Little Bavaria. Gus bought a little bag of lemon drops then offered some to Burt and Cecily when they walked to the next store.

Most of their time was spent window shopping, Gus and Burt staying outside while Cecily ran in to check the price on an item or to see what else they had in stock. Although they did find a craft beer store where Burt and Gus both purchased a few bottles of specialty ales they wanted to try later at home.

A while later, they were on the doorstep of the Cheese Haus, and Gus felt more than ready to go home. Burt seemed to be fading as well. Cecily studied a cold display case of imported cheeses and selected one. Gus leaned in and whispered to her. "I think Burt is about done for the day."

She agreed without looking over at him. "I figured. This will definitely be our last stop before we go home." She held up another cheese. "Want some of this goat cheese? It's on sale."

He wrinkled his nose at the thought. He'd never been much of a fan for anything goat. "I'm good."

She gave a shrug then put the cheese into her wooden basket before striding toward the front of the store. Gus stayed where he was and watched her go. A moment went by.

"Gus, could you give me a hand here?" Burt asked at one of the display cases.

Gus went to help him. "Find something you like?"

"I was just wondering the same thing about you." Pops pointed to a plastic container on a shelf above his head. "Glad and I always enjoyed some of that cheese dip. Would you mind grabbing me one?"

Gus plucked a container from the shelf and handed it to Burt. "This trip is bringing up a lot of good memories?"

Burt nodded. "Some of my best. You know, I only wish you'll have the same when you get to be my age. I'd hate for you to look back and regret those missed opportunities."

"I'm not missing anything, you old sea dog."

Pops gave a bark of laughter. "I don't mean those wild adventures you go on. Motorcycles and parachuting and such. I meant those quiet moments with the woman you love. The ones you wish that you could revisit and hold her one last time."

Gus put his hands on the wheelchair and pushed Burt forward, heading for the store's exit. He figured he'd be reliving that dance with Cecily. That time he'd held her in his arms for just a few special minutes. And how she'd sparkled as she laughed.

ON THE RIDE HOME, Burt insisted on sitting in the back seat and fell asleep shortly after Cecily pulled out of the parking lot of the restaurant. Gus saw her sneak a peek at her sleeping grandfather. "He's looking a little gray, isn't he?"

Gus turned to get a better look at Burt. The older man did appear worn out, and he could see the blue tinge of Burt's lips. Gus reached over and double-checked to make sure the portable oxygen machine was fully plugged into the USB port by the extra-long cord that reached the back seat. "Today wore him out, but I think it's a good kind of tired."

Cecily pursed her lips together, and Gus gently put his hand on hers. He removed his hand just as quickly as she turned to glare at him. He held up his hands to apologize for the action. "There are going to be good and bad days for Burt, but let's not go looking for the bad when it's been a good day."

Her shoulders sagged a little as if some of her tension had released, but he noticed that the tendons in her neck were still tight. He thought of how she shone when she smiled bright or the expression on her face when they crashed into each other on the dance stage. What he wouldn't do to go back to those moments. "It seemed to lift his spirits quite a lot."

He saw her eyes dart to the rearview mirror, then back to the road. "I can't help but worry about him. Besides my mom, he's the only family I've got."

"I thought Burt mentioned a grandson."

Cecily rolled her eyes. "My brother, you mean. He's…" She gave a shrug, then a quick shake of her head. "He's living out west pursuing his dream of being a standup comedian. He's convinced that he's one joke away from being the next comic sensation."

"I take it you don't believe that."

"He is a funny guy, but how long do you pursue something before you accept it's likely not going to happen? Five years? Ten?" Her disappointed look spoke volumes. "If you ask me, it's time for him to give up and come home."

"Tell me how you really feel." Gus turned to look at Cecily while she drove. "Are you upset because he's not successful in pursuing his dream or because that puts the brunt of your grandfather's care onto you and your mom?"

"BJ has always been about one person. Himself. He always has an excuse for why he can't come and see Pops. And I know it would do them both a lot of good if he did."

Gus felt the words hit his heart, and the guilt over his own grandfather reared its ugly head. "Sometimes you can't be there even though you want to."

"He's choosing not to be here."

Gus fell silent and turned his gaze out the window. "I couldn't be there for my granddad for years like I wanted to."

"Where were you?"

"I was stationed in Germany first. Then Virginia, Georgia and finally Texas. As well as a stint in Afghanistan."

"You were in the army. That's different."

"I could have left after my first four-year commitment, but I signed on again for another four. I wanted to see more of the world before I settled down." He turned back to look at her. "But if I could do it over, I'd have come home sooner. Maybe BJ feels the same."

Cecily scoffed at his words. "You don't know my brother like I do."

"Have you ever asked him to come home?"

"I have. But there's always an excuse."

"I understand how you're feeling, but I know what it's like to chase something that takes you away from your family for a while. And maybe there's more to the story than what you think you know."

Silence fell again in the car, the only sounds the soft music from the radio and the hum of the oxygen machine. "What were you chasing?" Cecily finally asked.

"I wanted to get away from the small town I grew up in, and the army seemed to provide the perfect outlet. Plus, I had ambitions of being a doctor and couldn't afford med school. The GI bill made it possible for me to go to college."

"I've been wondering how it is that you ended up a first responder."

Gus gave a soft chuckle. "I originally

thought I wanted to go to medical school. But then detoured into the military, although I did get training as a medic in the army, then later got my license as a paramedic. I'm a good guy to have around in an emergency." He looked down at his hands. "Or I was. I got burnt out on the job the last couple of years. So now I'm exploring other options."

"What kind of options?"

"Anything but medicine." He'd taken odd jobs in retail, food service and delivery to pay the bills. But he hadn't found his niche. Yet.

"But it's a noble profession."

"So is teaching. So is being a short-order cook. So is driving trucks that transport supplies across the state. There are a million jobs out there that can have as much meaning. I just haven't found the right one for me yet."

"Now you do sound like my brother."

And the comparison didn't sound favorable based on the dry tone in her voice. "Anyway, it's an amazing thing what you're doing, taking care of Burt."

"Even if you don't agree with my methods?"

"Especially then."

A strand of hair had fallen out of her ponytail and had gotten caught on her eyelashes. She reached up to push it away but missed. He wanted to tuck it behind her ear but stopped himself.

"I'm glad you didn't."

"Didn't what?"

"Touch me." Her grip tightened on the steering wheel. "It makes me confused."

That surprised him. He looked at her closer, trying to stop the smile on his lips. "I didn't realize that I confused you."

"It's not you. It's when you touch me."

"Then I won't do that. Unless you ask me to."

She gave a short laugh at this. "Trust me. I won't be asking you."

He couldn't keep the smile off his face this time. "I don't know about that. I might tempt you in ways that you can't even imagine right now."

She glanced in the rearview mirror. "Are you really flirting with me with my grandfather sitting there right in the back seat?"

"He's asleep. Besides, between you and me, I bet he's got matchmaking on his mind."

"Matchmaking?" This time her laughter sounded like the tinkling of tiny bells. "You think he's trying to get the two of us together?"

"He all but admitted it to me earlier today." He rested his arm along the inside edge of the passenger door. "Said I couldn't do better than you."

"Well, I certainly could do better than you." She gave him a quick side glance. "No offense."

Gus chuckled at that and gave a short nod. "You're probably right about that. I'm not the best boyfriend material."

"Why? Because you're not the marrying kind?"

"I wouldn't say that, since I've been married twice. But I'm not the lasting kind. Not like your grandfather, who was happily married for a hundred years."

"It was forty-two."

"You know what I mean, Cecily. I don't have the staying power to make a relationship last."

"Considering I just got divorced too, I

don't think I'm exactly the best candidate for being anyone's lasting girlfriend right now."

They drove the rest of the way home in silence.

CHAPTER THREE

CEC FOLLOWED THE highway at the exit that would take them home. That left about a half hour more to go, give or take. She eyed her passenger and found him asleep, his head drooped to the side, eyes closed, mouth slightly open. The sight made her lips twitch in an almost smile. He looked pretty cute that way.

Then she glanced in the rearview mirror at Pops. He too still slept, his body sagging to the right and his head resting on the closed window. He still looked a little gray, so she leaned over and checked the connection between the portable oxygen machine and the USB port. It was secure and in as tight as it would go. The pack rested beside Pops in the back seat, so she couldn't reach and turn up the outflow.

Maybe they should have stayed home.

But the look on Pops's face as their server

brought that large platter of chicken to their table had been worth it. So had the joy on Pops's face after she and Gus had been dancing.

On the other hand, this little road trip could set him back. It had clearly worn him out completely.

And yet, he'd seemed more alive while they'd been in Little Bavaria than he had in weeks. He'd had good color then in his cheeks. His spirits had been high. He'd looked great. Happy.

But what if the cost of that happiness was that he got sicker faster?

She shook her head as if her brain was a snow globe that would make the negative thoughts disappear and let the positive ones float down and take hold.

She couldn't help worrying about Pops. He had stepped into the role of father when hers had died. She'd had more years with Pops than she'd had with her dad. And at times, she couldn't remember her dad. Would she slowly forget Pops too? Not in big chunks, but bits at a time. The sound of his booming laugh. The smell of his soap. The rough feel of his cheek against hers.

She shook her head again. He wasn't dead yet. He was still here, which is why the day had been so important. But it had gone by so quickly, and they were almost home, their adventure over.

After she pulled into the driveway and then into the garage, she put a hand softly on Gus's bare arm. "Hey, we're home."

He blinked at her, then took a deep breath as he stretched. "How long have I been sleeping?"

"Not quite an hour."

He gave a nod, then turned in the seat to check on Pops. "Burt slept the whole way home too?"

"He probably needed the rest."

"He's going to need help getting in the house, so I'll do that first and then give you a hand to unpack the car."

"Why do you think he's going to need help? He's been fine walking on his own." Gus gave her a look that seemed to say he knew more than she did. She waited a beat and he finally said, "Okay. I'll go unlock the door. We can go in through the kitchen."

She grabbed her purse before exiting the car and walking to the recently installed ramp that led from the garage into the house. The ramp would become increasingly necessary to keep Pops mobile. The doctor had said there would come a time when he wouldn't be able to walk anymore and would have to use the wheelchair full-time. As much as Pops complained about the thing, it would be handy to have around.

She propped the door open, then returned to the car where Gus helped Pops up. He held on to him at the waist. "Steady, now?" she asked.

Pops grunted, and Gus kept his arm around Pops's waist. "Just a few steps to the ramp. You think you can make it on your own?"

"I'm no baby."

"No, but you're tired and a little weak, right?" Gus hung on to him.

Pops yawned. "I just need to wake up a little."

"Why don't I help you to your bedroom?"

"No. Get me to my chair in the living room."

Pops took a step, faltered and then claimed Gus's arm.

Gus leaned into her grandfather and

braced him on one side. "I'll help you get there, okay?"

"Do what you want."

While Cec followed, the two men walked slowly to the ramp, up and into the house, then through the kitchen to the living room where Pops's recliner waited. With a groan, Pops let go of Gus and fell back into the chair. "This chair never felt so good."

Cec took a throw blanket that her grandmother had crocheted long ago and placed it over Pops. "Why don't you get more rest while Gus and I unload the car?"

"Don't forget the chicken in the cooler."

She smiled, then bent and gave him a kiss on his whiskery cheek. "How could I forget?"

"And that blueberry jam too. Gonna be good on my toast tomorrow morning."

Gus returned with her to the garage. He started to lift the oxygen tanks from the trunk and place them with the others against one of the garage walls. Cec approached him. "How did you know he was going to be so weak after today?"

"I've noticed he's getting tired more easily. And his balance has been off." Gus reached for another tank. "Has he fallen yet?"

"Just the one time this winter before he got diagnosed."

Gus nodded and continued emptying her trunk. "When it starts happening again, I want you to call me. I'll come help him up. You won't be able to lift him on your own."

"I'm stronger than I look."

"I'm sure you are, but Burt is hardly a small man. And he won't be able to do much to help you lift him. It may get to a point where I can't lift him on my own either. It's going to take the two of us."

"You talk like it's inevitable."

"Burt is a proud man, so having to rely on you and me for what he used to do on his own is going to be tough. He could get stubborn and try to do things by himself."

"You mean, more stubborn than he already is?"

"And that could make him angry. He might even get belligerent and take it out on you. But it's not you he's angry with. It's the disease."

"How do you know so much about this?"

"Part of my training. And I've seen it

time and again with terminal patients." Gus paused and turned to face her. "It's going to get really rough. But you don't have to do this on your own. I can help you out as much as I can. I'm right next door. You only have to call me."

"My mom said she will move in and help me out too when the time comes. Right now, she's working nights at the hospital which makes it difficult for her, but she stops in when she can."

"Good." He nodded and took out the cooler before walking back into the kitchen. Cec stared after him, wondering why he had felt like she needed a lecture.

CECILY JOINED HIM in the kitchen as he emptied out the cooler, placing the items on the closest counter. Gus didn't know where things went , although he knew better than to try and guess. Everyone had their own quirks when it came to kitchen organization.

She came up beside him. "I can take care of this. You did enough."

He guessed that was his cue to leave. "I'll tell Burt goodbye then."

He'd felt bad having to tell Cec what to

expect with Burt's eventual decline. But he wasn't sure what she knew and worried she hadn't thought about what the coming weeks and months were going to bring. Better to be prepared than blindsided.

When he entered the living room, he found that Burt had turned on the television, but the older man had fallen back asleep. He debated whether to wake him up to say goodbye, but Burt opened his eyes. "I'm not sleeping."

Gus gave him a smile, then took a seat on the sofa beside him. "Cec has got everything under control here, so I'm going back to my house. Maybe catch the last few innings of the baseball game."

Burt nodded toward the television screen. "They're down by two."

"They still have plenty of time to pull out a victory." Gus put his arm on the older man's shoulder. "You should get plenty of rest the next couple of days. You'll probably need it."

"I'm fine."

Gus gave him a look, and the older man gave a shrug. "Okay, I'm tired but nothing new with that."

"I'll be back tomorrow night with a new beer I found. It's an IPA with a cherry finish."

"Why they started putting fruit into beer, I'll never understand."

Gus chuckled, then shook his head. "I'm betting you'll like it. I hope." Burt gave a grumble, but Gus could tell it was half-hearted at best. He patted the man's shoulder again before rising to his feet. "Get some rest, you old sea dog"

"Be careful with that old business, grunt."

Gus smiled as he reentered the kitchen to find Cecily standing at the counter, staring down at the bird ornament that Burt had purchased at the Christmas store. Her eyes and cheeks were dry, but he could tell that they would dampen once he left her alone. He crossed the room and stood next to her. "I told Burt to get some rest, but maybe it's good advice for you too."

She glanced up at him as if just realizing he hadn't left the house. "Rest. Yes, I will." She looked back down at the ornament, then slowly rewrapped it in the tissue paper she'd taken it out of.

"He bought it to comfort you."

"I know." She put the ornament back into the box and slid it further down the counter. "Thank you for all your help today. We couldn't have gone without you."

"You probably wanted to leave me behind, but I'm glad you included me."

She gave a nod, then turned to grab a glass from a cabinet and filled it with water from the faucet. "I've got to give Pops his medication."

"I'll see you tomorrow night."

She turned off the faucet. "What's tomorrow night?"

"Bringing Burt some more craft beer to try. I was thinking if you want to go out with a friend or something, then I can stay here with Burt while you're gone. I know you haven't had much of a chance to get out lately." The older man would soon get to the point where leaving him alone wouldn't be an option. Not that Cecily or Burt seemed ready to accept that fact yet.

"I don't have any plans tomorrow night, so I'll be here."

Gus gave a nod. "Until then." He left her kitchen and took the back door through the garage and crossed the driveway to get to his house next door, entering through the side door. Inside, it was hushed. Dark despite the evening sun still shining brightly. He hadn't thought to open the blinds in the kitchen before he'd left earlier that day. Crossing his kitchen now, he opened them and glanced around the room. His house was a mirror image of Burt's. But his felt emptier. Quieter.

Lonelier.

Gus sighed and ran a hand over his face. Time to find a hobby or something that would occupy his attention and fill this emptiness.

He left the kitchen and entered the living room, pausing briefly to turn on the television to the ball game. Ah, noise. He turned the volume up a few notches then collapsed onto his sofa.

He stretched out, then placed an arm over his eyes. An image of Cecily laughing as they danced surfaced, then fled just as quickly. Yep. Time to find a hobby before he did something ill-advised like fall for his neighbor's granddaughter.

CEC HELPED POPS to bed later that night.

She handed him the last of his evening

pills and waited while he chased them with a glass of water. He passed her the empty glass, then tried to swing his legs into bed. After two failed attempts, she placed the glass on the nightstand then lifted his legs and pulled the covers over him.

"I hate this getting old business."

She leaned in and kissed his forehead. "I'd rather you get old than the alternative."

"Easy for you to say." He gave a yawn. "That was fun today, wasn't it?"

"Yes. I'm glad we went."

"So, what's next?"

"You have another doctor's appointment on Friday and then Dr. Buddy next week. And they're delivering another shipment of oxygen tanks early next week. Tuesday maybe."

"Bah. You know what I mean. Where are we going next?"

"Right now, you are going to sleep, and I'll be doing that myself soon. It's been a long day for the both of us."

Pops propped himself up on one elbow. "I don't want this to be the end of our journeys."

"Why don't you get a good night's sleep

before we talk about another adventure?" She picked up the glass from the nightstand.

"I mean it, baby girl. There's still more of the world I want to see before I'm gone."

"We can discuss it in the morning."

Pops lay back on the bed, and Cec walked to the door. She turned to look at him. "You sleep in as long as you need to tomorrow, okay? There's nothing on the calendar, and I think we both deserve it."

"You certainly do. Love you."

"Love you too." She gave him a smile and then stepped out of the room, closing the door behind her.

She returned to the kitchen and straightened it up, wiping down the counters and starting the dishwasher. It wasn't full, but there wouldn't be room for the next day's dishes if she didn't run it that evening. She wrung out the dishrag, then hung it over the middle partition of the double sink. The hooting of an owl brought her attention to the window, and she glanced outside at the still-bright sky. It would stay light out until almost ten now that they were at the beginning of summer. She liked the long, warm days. Especially since there was lots of time before she needed to start planning the upcoming curriculum.

A light in the kitchen window across from hers turned on, and she could see Gus enter and head to the refrigerator. Afraid that he'd catch her staring at him, she took a step to the side, away from the window. But then curiosity got to her, and she leaned over to peek. He still stood staring into the refrigerator. But then, as if he sensed her there, he spotted her.

Cec took a step back and rested her head against the cabinet. What was she doing? What had changed since that morning? Gus was still the opinionated neighbor and friend of her grandfather. And yet...

Dancing with him to the oompah band had altered something between. The mood? How she saw him? Talking with him in the garage about Pops had altered it further. And now, she didn't know what it was exactly that she was supposed to feel. Or think. Or do. It had seemed like they had become a team. Almost.

She peeked around the cabinet to find the light off in Gus's kitchen. She pressed her fingers to her forehead. Tired. That's what she was. And what she needed to do was go to bed and forget how, for just a moment, she'd been tempted by the sight of Gus gazing at his leftovers.

THE DAY AFTER their visit to Little Bavaria, Pops slept most of the day. Cec found it quiet, and very lonely to tiptoe around the house so she wouldn't disturb him as he rested in his recliner. She had thought about tackling some cleaning, but she didn't want to run the vacuum and interrupt his nap or start tidying up the basement and not hear his call if he needed her.

As a result, she spent most of her day on her phone playing games or looking at social media apps. She almost jumped when her cell phone started to ring. A look at the screen told her it was her brother. "Hey, BJ. How was your gig last night?"

"Thanks, you remembered." He paused. "I tried out some new material, but it didn't quite grab the audience like I'd hoped."

"That's the way it goes some times. Gotta stay positive."

BJ sounded defeated. "It's frustrating, you know? I could really make it big out here, but… I don't know. I feel like maybe it's time that I give up and move back home."

Snippets of her conversation with Gus came to mind. True, she'd been a little harsh about her brother, but she still loved the guy. "What are you talking about? You're the funniest person I know."

"If I'm so funny, then why haven't I broken out like some of the people I know. They even came out here at the same time. You remember my roommate Steve? He just signed on to do a sitcom development deal. And that woman I dated, Heather? She got hired on to write for a popular late-night show." He blew out a burst of air. "Everyone seems to be doing really well. Everyone but me."

"You were featured in that young comics to watch article that you sent Mom. That's got to mean something. And didn't you say that an agent came to see your show and gave you advice on how to improve?"

"I don't know what to do."

She tried to figure out how to bring up the topic of Pops and chose to jump right in. "Listen, Pops isn't doing so well. Maybe you should consider coming back for a short visit. You could catch up with him and take a break from the Hollywood scene. Might give you a fresh perspective when you go back."

"I'm not sure, Cec."

She bit back an angry retort and closed her eyes, reminding herself that he loved Pops just as much as she did. "He misses you."

"I miss him too, but I hate seeing him so sick. It's not fair. Especially since we lost Dad to the same stupid disease."

This time she couldn't stop the words. "None of us like seeing him this sick, but time is running out, BJ. He wants to see you."

When he didn't refuse, she pushed forward. "If it's a money thing, I can send you a plane ticket."

"I can't ask you to do that."

"You're not asking. I'm offering." She gripped the phone tighter in her hand. "Consider it an early birthday gift then. Please think about coming home. You don't want to miss a chance to say goodbye."

Silence. "He's getting that bad?"

"I tell you what. Think about my offer, and I'll call you in a few days."

"Is he there? I'd like to talk to him."

"I'll check to see if he's awake." She looked over at Pops to find him looking at her. "Here he is."

She handed the phone over to him. Pops greeted BJ, then laughed at something her brother said. She settled back into the sofa when a knock on the front door captured her attention.

Gus was standing on the front porch, his head turned to look behind him at a kid on a bicycle who raced by, calling his name. He held up a hand, then turned back to her. "Can Burt come out to play?"

"Funny. He's on the phone with BJ."

"Ahh, the absent brother." Gus held up a six-pack of craft beer. "I came over as promised."

She took a step aside so that Gus could enter. As he passed by her, she noticed the scent of soap linger after him and saw the wet wisps of hair at the base of his neck. Maybe he'd had a lazy day also.

In the living room, Gus took a seat on the sofa and gave a small wave to Burt who nodded and shortly wrapped up the phone conversation. "That was BJ. He's talking about maybe coming back home for a visit."

Cec hoped that was a good sign that he would take her up on her offer. Pops looked at the case in Gus's hands. "What did you bring me?"

He took one of the bottles and handed it to Pops. "It's that cherry one I told you about."

Pops twisted the cap off and took a long swig before rubbing the back of his hand across his mouth. "I hate to say it, but that does taste pretty good."

Cec rubbed her eyes. "What time is it?"

"Almost seven."

How long had she been wasting while on her phone? The last time she looked at her watch had been four or four thirty when Glenda from across the street had dropped off a couple of books she'd finished reading and thought Pops might be interested. She groaned. "I never made us dinner tonight. I slept right through."

Gus held out a bottle of beer toward her. "Sounds like you needed the rest more than food."

Cec waved the beer away and rose to her

feet. "I can throw together a salad really quick to go with the leftover chicken from yesterday. Is that okay, Pops?"

He made a face and took another long pull of beer before belching softly. "I'm okay with this."

"But you haven't eaten much today. And it's too late to defrost anything."

Gus pulled out his phone and started tapping. "Don't worry. I've got it covered. Do you prefer pepperoni or sausage?"

"Now that you mention it, I could go for a pizza. Sausage and green peppers," Pops answered.

"No pizza. It gives you heartburn and it will keep you up all night." She held up a hand to Gus. "Thank you, but no thank you."

"Baby girl, let me live a little. I haven't had pizza in more than four months."

"Exactly. Not since I moved in. I remember how sick you got." She turned back to Gus. "No pizza."

Gus looked over at Pops who gave a shrug. "I guess no pizza."

Gus put his phone back into the pocket of his jeans and claimed a seat on the sofa. He took a bottle of beer and opened it. "Well, we gotta eat. If not pizza, what? Wings? Subs?"

"We've got plenty of leftovers from yesterday. I could reheat some of the sides we brought home and serve those?" She had to feed her grandfather something, his care was her responsibility.

"Fine." Pops took another swig of beer then gave a decisive nod. "We'll have chicken. And those tasty sides."

In the kitchen, she pulled out plates and set the table for three since Gus seemed intent on joining them. She could hear the two men talking in the other room. Once she had reheated the chicken, dressing and noodles, plus a little tub of gravy, and placed them on the table along with some cranberry relish, she called out for the others to join her. It took a while for them to enter the room, Pops leading the way, shuffling along with his walker, Gus behind him.

"How are you feeling today, Burt?" Gus asked as they started to pass dishes around the table.

"Fine."

Gus looked at Cec, who shook her head. "He's been sleeping all day."

"Looks like you did your fair share of that too." Gus pointed to her hair then passed her the cranberry relish, his finger briefly touching hers.

She ignored the zing and took a spoonful. "I didn't mean to fall asleep, so I guess yesterday wore the both of us out." She tried to straighten her hair.

"I'm not worn out." When they turned to look at Pops, he gave a shrug. "What? I sleep a lot already, so it's not like that's something new."

He set the bowl of noodles down in the middle of the table. "Which is why I'd like to bring something up with the two of you. I'd like to make another road trip."

"I don't know about that, Pops."

Gus shrugged. "Where do you want to go this time?"

Pops set his fork down and took his time before speaking. "I want to go back to Lighthouse Bay. The town I grew up in."

CHAPTER FOUR

GUS HAD NEVER heard of Lighthouse Bay, but from the look on Cecily's face it wasn't a day trip there and back like Little Bavaria. He glanced between them. "Where's that?"

Cecily just shook her head at Burt. "No. We're not going there. It's too far."

"We could do it in a few days if we take lots of breaks." Burt glanced at Gus. "You don't mind making another road trip with us, do you?"

Cecily continued shaking her head and crossed her arms over her chest. "There's no way in the world that this is going to work. It's in the middle of nowhere. Do they even have a doctor nearby if something should happen?"

Burt huffed. "It's not Siberia, so I'm sure they have medical care if it's an emergency."

Gus looked between them and put his hands up in a T to indicate a timeout in their two-way argument. "Where are we talking about exactly?"

Cecily finally looked over at him. "The northern tip of the Upper Peninsula of Michigan on the shores of Lake Superior. It's as far north that you can get in our state before you enter Canada." She turned back to Burt. "I agreed to let you go to Little Bavaria..."

"*Let me*?"

"...because we wouldn't be that far away if something... unfortunate happened, but there is no way in the world that we're going to drive twelve hours..."

"It's closer to ten," Pops pointed out.

"Well, it might as well be a hundred because you are not going." Cecily stood and tossed her napkin on the table. She stalked to the kitchen and stared out the window over the sink.

Gus looked across the table at Burt. "Why do you want to go back to your hometown?"

The older man didn't say anything for a moment but stared at Cecily's back. Finally, he sighed and turned to look at Gus. "I've been thinking about home for a while now. Maybe getting closer... to the end makes me sentimental about my life and about things I wish I could have done differently. Go back to the beginning to figure out how I ended up where I am."

"What do you have there? Family? Friends? A girl you left behind?"

Burt gave a shrug and a soft smile. "My family moved away from there years ago. And she's probably long gone from there now, too."

Gus gave a low whistle. "So, there was a girl. Did you ever look her up?"

Cecily turned to glare at them. "Do not encourage him. Because we are not going. Period."

Gus ignored her and kept his focus on Burt. "We could see if she's on social media. Maybe she's still living there."

"If she is, then she's probably married. A woman like her doesn't stay available for long." Burt took a deep breath and released it. "Maybe Cec is right. This is a ridiculous idea."

Cecily returned to stand behind her chair, clutching the back of it so tightly that her knuckles turned white. "You're right that it's ridiculous. And you'd be wrong if you think that your doctor will sign off on letting you go on some harebrained trip up north."

Burt looked up at her. "And what if I do get her to agree that I could go? Would you change your mind then?"

"Nothing will convince me that it's a good idea."

Gus spoke softly. "Burt brings up a good point. What if we could get Dr. Buddy to give him the clearance to go on an extended trip? When is your next appointment, Burt?"

"Next week." Burt looked at Cecily as if to get confirmation.

She nodded. "But there is no way that she will agree. As it is, we see her every other week. And if it's not her, it's the respiratory therapist. Or the hospice nurse. Or the social worker." She walked to a calendar that hung on the wall and waved a hand across it as if she was a spokesmodel on television. "Your time is filled up with appointments that we can't miss. We're not going. End of discussion."

Burt pursed his lips, then rose to his feet and used his walker to leave the room. Cecily watched him go, her eyes more sad than upset. She collapsed into a chair and rested her head in her hands. Gus scooted the chair closer to her and put a hand on her arm, then quickly removed it, remembering how she'd said his touch confused her. "Don't beat yourself up."

She put her hands down and looked at him. "I'm not trying to be mean, but he doesn't understand that everything I'm doing is for his own good."

"Right now, all he sees is everything that he's lost. And not being able to go is just one more thing being taken away from him."

"So, what am I supposed to do? Agree to go with him and then he gets sick or worse?" She shook her head. "Going on a day trip is one thing, but we're talking at least a week with all the driving back and forth."

"But what if the doctor says it would be okay for him to go? Shouldn't we give him this chance?"

"We?"

Gus gave a shrug. "I'm just as invested in this as you are. Burt is my friend, and I would do what I have to do in order to help him get what he wants."

She gave him an odd look, but then sighed. "Fine. We'll see what the doctor says. If she says he can make the trip, then we'll go."

"Yes!" Burt's voice came from the living room.

Cecily rolled her eyes. "I knew he was listening." She raised her voice and said, "But if she says that it's a no-go, then that's all there is to it. No trip."

THE DOCTOR HAD Pops put his shirt back on after listening to his lungs. "There's a crackling sound in the left lung that I didn't notice on the last visit."

Cec perched on the edge of her chair. "Is that bad?"

Dr. Buddy looked up from her tablet where she'd been typing. "Could be extra fluid buildup, but your grandfather has had the crackling before, and it went away on its own. We'll have to monitor it." She studied Pops. "How do you feel otherwise?"

"Like a truck ran over me twice and is backing up to make a third run at me. So pretty much the same as the last dozen times you've asked me."

Dr. Buddy smirked but wrote the comment down on the tablet as Burt buttoned up his shirt and made a motion to Cec. She knew what he wanted, but she didn't want to bring up the proposed road trip. Finally, Pops cleared his throat. "Actually, there's something my granddaughter would like to discuss with you."

"You could have asked her yourself, you know." She turned to the doctor. "Pops would like to travel to the Upper Peninsula to visit the town where he grew up. With all the appointments and care that he requires plus being on oxygen, I'm not so sure that it's a good idea. But I promised that we would ask you your opinion whether this is something he could do."

Dr. Buddy focused again on Pops. "What part of the UP?"

"Little town called Lighthouse Bay. You ever been?"

"Can't say I have. But my son will be a freshman at Michigan Tech this fall, so I'm sure I'll be seeing more of the state up there."

"It's beautiful. Untouched."

"It is that."

Cec crossed her arms over her chest. "It's

also remote and really far away from here. I'm worried that my grandfather won't get the care he needs if we're not here."

The doctor nodded and placed the tablet on the stool she'd been sitting on earlier. "Can I be frank with the two of you? The best that I can do for Burt at this point is to make him comfortable. I can't cure you or fix you. There's nothing more I have to offer. So, if a trip like this is important to you, Burt, and if you take the necessary precautions, then I can't find a reason to keep you here. In fact, it might do you a little good."

Pops shot Cec a victory look, and she bristled. "And what if something happens while we're up there?"

"They have medical facilities up there like we do here. And be sure to take my contact information just in case." She smiled at Pops. "So, when were you thinking of going on this trip?"

"As soon as possible."

Dr. Buddy gave Cec a few prescriptions that she would need to pick up later from the pharmacy and then released them. Pops took his time using his walker to leave the room, and Cecily held back to catch the doctor for a moment alone. "Are you really sure the trip is okay for him? He's getting so weak. And his breathing is getting worse. You already said we need to increase the volume of oxygen that he's receiving."

"He's never going to get better than what he is right now, Cecily. Time is running out for him, that's the bottom line."

"All the more reason to not go." She peered at the doctor. "Am I right?"

"Actually, I'd argue that it's the opposite. As I said before, the trip could be beneficial to him, maybe give him closure on something, or maybe just happy memories. It's only going to get tougher on you both the closer we get to the end. Having some good times to hold on to will buoy your spirits on those bad days." The doctor put her hand on Cec's arm. "But it is better for him if you take this trip soon. Don't wait."

Gus TYPED THE name into the search engine as Burt looked over his shoulder. "Do you think we could find her?"

"If she's active on social media, sure."

"And if she's still alive." Burt pointed at

a name, Phyllis Lennon. "Click on her. Her maiden name was Lennon."

"I thought you said she got married."

"Sure, but maybe they got divorced or he died, and she took her name back." Burt shook his head as the woman's picture came up on the screen. "Nope. That's not her."

"It's been over sixty years since you last saw her. How do you know it's not?"

Burt pushed his glasses forward on the tip of his nose and got closer to the screen. "She doesn't have the sparkle in her eyes that my Phyllis had. Trust me. It's not her."

Burt ran his finger down the screen names that had popped up in the search engine and pointed to another. "This might be her. Phyllis1203. Her birthday is December third."

But again, it wasn't the woman that Burt remembered. Gus had doubts that Burt would be able to recognize the woman after all these years, but they looked at several more profiles searching for Phyllis. Burt leaned back on the sofa, seemingly resigned.

Gus asked, "Are you okay?"

"Tired more than usual." The older man

closed his eyes. "I know my granddaughter thinks I'm silly for wanting to go on this trip, but she doesn't understand why it's important to me."

Gus put the laptop to the side. "Why is it important?"

Burt opened his eyes. "The closer I get to not being here anymore, the more I want to go back to where it all started. I want to see the house where I was born. The school I went to. To walk down the same streets I did as a boy."

"So, you want to relive your childhood?"

"Not relive it so much as visit it one last time. And if I could see Phyllis and tell her..." Burt sighed and waved a hand through the air as if erasing what he had been about to say. "Never mind. We're never going to find her. And she's probably one of those people who moved south when she retired. She always liked the warm weather."

"My guess is that's because you didn't get that much of it that far north."

Burt laughed. "You're right about that. Going swimming in Lake Superior was taking a chance that you'd freeze a body part off even if it was mid-August in the middle of a heat wave."

Gus picked up the laptop and put more information in the search engine. "Let's narrow our search to every Phyllis who lives in Michigan. If we strike out on all of those, we'll broaden our search area."

"You think she stayed?"

"You did. Maybe she did too. If she has grandchildren, she might not have wanted to move away, no matter how hot it is in Florida." He angled the screen so that Burt could read through the names. "We can start with the first one and go down from there until we find her."

They must have clicked on several dozen names until Burt tapped his finger on the screen. "That's her! I swear it on my life, that's my Phyllis."

Phyllis Graham listed her location as Copper Harbor, which Burt informed Gus was close to Lighthouse Bay. "Close enough that you could put one foot in each town." The older man gave him a big grin. "She's still a looker, isn't she? After all these years, she still takes my breath away." He put a hand up to the back of his head.

"I'm going to have to get a haircut before we go. You think you could help me take care of that detail?"

"Of course. But don't you think you should write to her first? We could send her a message and see if she remembers you. Maybe even let her know that we'll be coming up there soon so the two of you can meet."

"Oh no, I couldn't do that. What if she doesn't want to see me? What if she's still angry at me for leaving her behind?"

"Wouldn't you like to find that out first before we go searching for her in Copper Harbor or Lighthouse Bay?"

"She's a bonus reason for the trip, not the main one."

Gus paused. "So, what's the real reason then?"

"It doesn't matter." Burt was trying to sound casual, but it wasn't working.

"It obviously does if you're willing to risk your health to go up north."

Burt gave a shake of his head. "It's not something I want to share just yet." He angled the laptop to look at the screen. "Do you think she'll want to meet for dinner or something?"

"The worst thing you can do is ask and she says no." Gus nudged the laptop closer to him. "Send her a message. Take a chance."

CEC DROPPED THE stack of books on the kitchen table, then sank into a chair. "I think I emptied the Thora library of all their books on the Upper Peninsula, but they didn't have anything specifically on Lighthouse Bay." She held up one. "Outdoor sports." And another. "Bed and breakfasts." And a few more. "Day trip suggestions. Restaurants. Shopping. All geared for the tourist." She peered across the table at Pops, who had selected a book and was flipping through it. "But something tells me we're not going to be visiting the places for tourists."

Pops shook his head. "Lighthouse Bay was pretty sparse when I was growing up."

"It's been over sixty years since you left. Did you ever go back to visit your hometown when you got out of the navy?"

"Once. But it didn't go well."

"Why not?"

"My family wasn't living there anymore. Soon after I left for the navy, my dad moved the family to Detroit to get a better job when the mines closed. And without my family there, the place didn't feel like home anymore."

"Which is why you moved here after college."

"My dad had taken a job at one of the car factories around here, and family is important." He reached over and patted her hand. "I wouldn't want to go through these last four years without you or your mom."

"So, what happened when you went back? What made it so bad?"

"You can never reclaim what you lost. And trying to change that only leads to sorrow."

"Did you look up your friends while you were there? Maybe an old girlfriend?"

"Most of them had moved on by then, so there wasn't many to try and find." He chose another book and flipped through it. "We don't need any of these books."

"Of course we do. We need to plan our route and where we're going to stay. True, I'll check out websites for more updated information, but this is a good place to start."

"I know Lighthouse Bay."

"Correction. You knew that town a long time ago, but I'm sure it's changed."

Pops shifted in his chair. "Maybe. But I still say we don't need these books. Let's just get in the car and see what happens."

"I'd feel better if we structured our days to get the most out of our time there." She selected one of the books and scanned a few pages. She'd feel better if they weren't going at all, but Pops seemed determined to go.

"I know you don't agree with my choice to visit there, but I'm glad you'll be going with me all the same."

She reached across the table and grabbed his hand, squeezing it. "I'd do anything if it could help you feel better."

"Well, I don't know if this trip will make me feel better, but it certainly won't make me feel worse."

That remained to be seen, in her opinion.

The doorbell rang, and Cec jumped up and went to answer it. Her mom, Anna, stood on the porch holding a folder in her hand along with her purse. "Hey, Mom, I didn't expect to see you today. Did your day off change?"

"Burt asked if I'd come over. He didn't tell you?"

She shook her head and held the screen door open wider. "Must have slipped his mind. Come on in. We're sitting in the kitchen talking about the road trip."

Her mom passed by her and walked back to the kitchen to greet Burt. "The one you just went on or the one coming up? Oh, hey, Dad, you seem to have a little more color in your face than the last time I saw you." She leaned over and kissed his cheek.

"Flattery will get you everywhere."

She rubbed his shoulder, then took the chair next to his and pointed to the stack of books. "What's all this then?" She picked up a book. "I see Cecily thinks she can plan every step of your next adventure."

"She wouldn't be Cecily if she didn't at least try."

They both turned to look at her, and Cec walked to a kitchen cupboard and opened it, bringing out three glasses. "I just made some iced tea with mint. Would you both like some?"

She put ice cubes in each glass, then filled them with tea before bringing them to the table. She took a sip then looked at her mother and Pops. "What? I just think it's better if we're prepared. There's nothing wrong with that."

"And there's nothing wrong with allowing room for spontaneity." Her mother gave her a familiar pointed look over the rim of her glass before taking a long sip of her iced tea.

Cecily rolled her eyes. More like failing to plan and following your whim. There was nothing wrong with making sure you had all the contingencies covered. And if they were really going on this trip, then she wanted to make sure she knew every possible issue that could come up and several solutions for each. This is what kept her awake at night. Imagining being so far from home, and Pops getting sicker or worse.

What if this gave her even less time with the man who meant so much to her? It was a selfish thought, she knew, but she couldn't stop herself. What would she do when he was gone?

She closed her eyes for a moment, then picked up a pen. "I want to make some notes. Just in case." She looked up to find Pops and her mom watching her. "Why are you both acting like I'm making a big mistake?"

Pops cleared his throat, which led to a bout of coughing. Cec ran to get a box of tissues and placed them on the table. He thanked her, then took a tissue and wiped his eyes and mouth. "I hate this. These attacks are getting worse."

"You're only proving my point that we should stay home." She found the section about emergency services in the area where they would be staying the longest and read.

"Sweetie, your grandfather and I want to talk to you about something. Could you put the planning on hold for just a moment?"

Cec looked up from the book and then set it aside, placing her finger in the margin to keep her spot. "Sounds serious."

Her mom glanced at Pops, then nodded. "I've been talking to Burt about what he wants when it comes to…the end, and we wanted to share it with you in case something does happen while you're away. And since you have medical proxy for him, it's important that you are aware of these wishes."

It felt like all the breath had left her body. She put a hand to her throat and then asked, "Pops, what is it that you want?"

He slid the folder, the one her mother had brought, across the table toward her. "I've spelled it all out in there. Your mom agreed to get the necessary forms from the hospital, and I have a notary who will be coming over in a little bit to make it official."

Cec frowned as she took the folder and opened it. "A medical directive?"

"Lays out how I want decisions over my care to be made."

She read through it, then stared at him. "Do not resuscitate. Do not intubate. Is this a joke?"

He shook his head. "I know what you're thinking…"

"No, you don't. Because if you did, you wouldn't ask me to helplessly watch you fight for air when the doctors could step in and help you." She closed the folder and slid it back across the table. "So, you're giving up? Not even going to fight it anymore?"

"Sweetie…"

"How could you let him agree to do this, Mom? You're basically taking away all his chances to live."

"This is his choice to make. Not mine or yours."

She gazed at her grandfather, who had once been the strongest man she had ever known. The one who had been in her life the longest. "This is you giving up."

"There's nothing more they can do."

"Because you have to be willing to fight."

"I'm tired of fighting. I don't have it left in me."

She blinked away the tears that threatened to fall down her cheeks. She couldn't show him sadness or weakness. Not now when she needed to be strong. "Then let me fight for you."

Pops took her hand in his. "This isn't your war. It's mine. Which makes this my decision."

She let her gaze fall to her lap. This couldn't be happening. Pops couldn't be expecting her to go along with this. "I don't know if I can agree to this."

"Agree or not, as my medical proxy, you

have to abide by my decisions in the directive."

She lifted her eyes and glared at him. "Then maybe I shouldn't be your proxy anymore. Since Mom seems to think you're right, maybe it should be her."

She rose to her feet and left the kitchen. In the backyard, the sun beat down on her bare arms, and she crossed them over her chest as she stared at the fence that bordered the property. She heard the sliding door open and shut but didn't turn around. It had to be her mother coming to tell her to grow up and go along with Pops's ludicrous ideas. "I know what you're going to say, and I don't want to hear it. This is not right. You know it."

But instead of her mother's voice, it was Gus who answered her. "Just because you don't agree with him, it doesn't make it wrong."

She turned to look at him. "You knew about this?" She cocked her head to the side. "Wait. You put him up to this."

"I only recommended that he consider his options and put them in writing so there's no question later on. His choices are his alone. You wouldn't want him to make choices over your life that you didn't agree with."

She brought a hand up to her forehead as she let the tears fall down her cheeks. "It's not fair."

Gus stepped forward and pulled her into his arms. "None of this is fair, Cecily."

"I don't want to lose him."

"I don't either. He's been the best friend I've ever had. And that's hard to find." He rubbed her back as she dampened the front of his T-shirt. "It's good to cry. Let it out."

She put her arms around his shoulders and gripped them tightly for a few minutes, holding on to him as if he were a lifeline in this tumultuous sea that Pops had thrown her into. Then realizing that this was Gus and being in his arms felt better than it should, she took a step back and wiped the tears from her face. "Sorry. I didn't mean to cry on you."

He ran a hand along the damp spot of his dark green shirt. "It's okay. This isn't my favorite T-shirt."

She opened her mouth to say something but realized she was going to apologize again when she already had. *But if I apologize again, maybe he'll put his arms around me again, and I'd really like to feel those strong arms around me one more time.* But that was a bad idea because they were about to spend a week or more on the road together. Why could she be turning to thoughts of romance when she should be thinking about Pops and that infernal document he expected her to uphold? "I better go back inside." She took a few steps, then turned back to Gus. "You know, you could have warned me that he was going to spring this on me."

"I honestly thought he had already told you."

She gave a nod and started walking away again. "And why did you come over today?"

"I found out some more information on Phyllis that I thought Burt might be interested in."

She froze and Gus almost bumped into her since he had been following her so closely. "Wait. Who is Phyllis?"

CHAPTER FIVE

ALTHOUGH SHE WAS invited to stay for dinner, Cecily's mom said she had plans to meet up with a friend before her shift at the hospital and had her daughter walk her out to her car. While they were gone, Gus asked, "How did it go?"

"Badly at first. But whatever you told her out in the backyard seemed to calm her down to at least listen to what I..." His words were cut off with a bout of coughing. He cleared his throat. "Can you pour me some more tea?"

Gus took the pitcher and filled Burt's glass and handed it to him. The older man gulped it down, then held his glass out again, his hand shaking a little. Gus poured him still more tea. "Thirsty?"

Burt nodded as he continued to guzzle. "But I think I need to switch to water."

"Are you getting enough fluids?"

"What are you? My nurse?" The old man sighed. "I drink my cup of coffee in the morning and then Cec forces me to drink something every once in a while. Don't tell her this, but I'm not a big fan of iced tea. And water has no taste."

"So, what will you drink?"

Burt gave a shrug then looked up at Cec, who returned to the kitchen with red-rimmed eyes. She gave a nod to them both, then walked to the counter. "I'm making taco salad for dinner. Gus, are you staying?"

"If it's no problem. I'd be happy to dice or chop."

"No need. You sit and talk with Pops about Delores."

"Phyllis," both men answered at once, then turned and smiled at each other.

Pops pointed at Gus. "You told her then?"

Gus gave a shrug. "A bit. I thought you had already filled her in."

"I wanted to wait until we knew more."

Cec had the fridge door open. "Whatever her name is, you guys talk. I'll cook."

Gus watched Cecily avoid their gaze as she brought out a package of ground beef, then rummaged around in a lower cabinet for a skillet. He enjoyed watching her bustle around, until he turned to find Burt looking at him. Back to Phyllis and quick, he thought. "Where's your laptop?"

"By my chair in the living room."

Gus retrieved the computer and set it up on the kitchen table. He brought up the website he'd found earlier that afternoon. "It appears that Phyllis and her husband own the general store in Lighthouse Bay." He angled the screen so that Pops could read it. "It was part of her husband's family for generations, and they took it over in the eighties. Phyllis runs it to this day with the help of her kids and grandkids."

Pops scrolled through the main page and clicked on a few tabs to read more. "Graham's Grocery and General Store. I remember that place. If they didn't have something, you had to drive for hours into Marquette and hope they had it there. But Mr. Graham tried to get everything you could think you might need." He pointed at a button on the screen. "It says you can order online, and it gets shipped to you. I wonder if they have her homemade rhubarb preserves." He smacked his lips. "I can still taste how good it was spread on toast. I'd give anything to have it one more time."

"If they don't sell it online, maybe we can pick some up when we're there."

"If she still makes it."

The sound of a knife whacking a cutting board brought their attention to Cecily, who attacked the lettuce as if it had done something to offend her. As Burt continued to peruse the website, Gus rose from his chair and joined her at the counter. "Everything okay?"

"Perfect," she answered, but continued to destroy the lettuce.

"Are you sure you don't want me to help you with something?" He looked toward the stove. "I think the beef is burning."

She gasped, then dropped the knife to grab a wooden spoon and stir the meat. Gus claimed the knife and took over her task of cutting lettuce into bite-size pieces before putting it in a large bowl. "It's okay to ask for help if you need it."

She kept her gaze on the skillet and broke up the chunks of beef into smaller pieces. "I was doing fine."

"Are you really fine though?"

She turned to him, a scowl on her face. "Yes." She looked at the lettuce in the bowl. "But as long as you're standing there, you might as well cut up the red pepper and onion."

He nodded and started slicing the pepper she had already washed while she added spices to the beef and stirred in a little water. He had enjoyed sharing the cooking duties with his first wife whenever he'd had the chance to. She was an excellent cook, and there were still times he missed her lasagna. For a long time, he'd missed her presence in their tiny apartment. The scent of her perfume that seemed to linger even when she wasn't there. The day it disappeared, he'd broken down and cried like a baby.

He sighed, and Cecily turned to look at him. "What's wrong?"

"Nothing. Just thinking about stuff." He gave her a smile. "What do you miss about your ex-husband?"

She turned her back to him and opened a can of black olives, then drained them in a colander that sat in the sink. "At the moment? Nothing."

"I find that hard to believe."

"Believe what you want, but I don't miss him. Or anything he used to do."

He didn't quite believe her but let that pass. "You must have had some good times with him. Tell me about one of them."

"Why?"

"Because I was thinking about how I miss my first wife's cooking, and I'd like to know that maybe she misses something about me. So, if you miss something about your ex, then maybe there's hope for me too."

Cecily's eyes bored into his for a moment, then she blinked. Seemed to soften. Letting down a piece of her armor that she had put in place to protect her. "I guess I miss the way he'd hold me while we watched television at night after dinner." A smile played around her lips. "Made me feel safe. Cherished, even."

Gus nodded. "That's a nice thing to remember."

"What do you miss about your second wife?" Cecily asked. He couldn't help the grin that seemed to come from somewhere deep inside. "The way she made me laugh.

She has the best sense of humor, and I loved it when she told me stories at the end of the day about the eccentric customers who visited the makeup counter where she worked."

"So why did you get divorced?"

"Because of the way she made me cry." He held up a tomato. "Wedges or diced?"

By the time dinner was ready and on the table Burt had discovered they didn't sell Phyllis's rhubarb preserves online, but they did have her strawberry rhubarb pie. He'd ordered one. "Just wait till you taste it, and you'll see for yourself how tasty it is."

Cecily passed Burt the bowl of salad first. "When is it supposed to be delivered?"

"By the end of next week."

"Won't we be on the road by then?" she asked, then stopped at Burt's astonished expression. "What? Are we only talking about making this road trip or are we actually going to go?"

"Do you mean it, baby girl?"

She nodded and handed him the jar of salsa. "Unless there's a reason we should delay our trip, I think we should leave sooner rather than later, like the doctor suggested." She turned to Gus. "What do you think?"

Gus noted the resignation on her face. She seemed to have decided to let go of her tight grip on Burt's health and let him make the decisions. He smiled at her, then turned to Burt. "Looks like you're going to have to cancel that pie order since we'll be picking it up in person. I have some things to take care of before I can go, but they won't take long. Why don't we leave Saturday morning?"

GUS PUSHED THE cart down the aisle at the grocery store as Cecily led the way to the snacks. She stopped in front of the chips and perused several choices before picking one kind and placing it in the cart. She turned to him. "These are Pops's favorite. What about you? Which ones do you want?"

He glanced at her. After spending time away from Cecily over the past few days, he'd hoped his attraction for Cecily would have cooled. But standing in the grocery store wearing a plain pink T-shirt and jean capris, she looked even better than he remembered. She had put her hair in a ponytail and wore little makeup. Cecily had a natural beauty that seemed to be effortless.

He blinked several times when he realized she expected an answer, then pointed to the sweet barbecue chips. "They've always been my favorite."

She picked up a bag and looked at it before turning to him. "I would have figured you for a spicy chip rather than a sweet one."

He shrugged. "What can I say? I've liked them since junior high."

She placed them in the cart and turned the corner. "We've got salty covered, but we do need sweet. Let's check the cookie aisle. Pops has been craving these sandwich crème cookies so much that I haven't been able to keep them in the house for very long."

In the cookie aisle, they found the sandwich cookies for Burt, and Gus added a bag of chocolate chip cookies to the cart as well. Cecily looked at the contents of the cart. "I want to make sure we have plenty of snacks for the trip, but two bags of chips and two packages of cookies doesn't seem enough for about a week or so." She turned to him. "What do you think?"

He thought the more time he spent with her, the more beautiful she became. Sure, she was uptight. And perhaps a bit obsessive with how she watched over Burt's health. But lovely all the same. "More is always better when it comes to snacks."

He followed her down another aisle. "So, you think we'll only be gone for a week?"

"That's what I'm planning on. Why? Do you need to be back sooner than that?" She stopped in front of the nuts and chose a can of mixed ones for the cart. "I think the granola bars are at the end of this aisle. And I want to pick up some fresh fruit."

"My plans are flexible so I can be gone longer if Burt needs it."

"What my grandfather needs is for us to go on this trip and get back as soon as possible."

"Why rush it? This is something he has set his heart on. Why not take the time for him to get everything accomplished that he wants to do?"

She detoured around a dad negotiating with two boys over which cereal to get.

"Do you know what his plans are? Because he's been vague when talking to me. It's not like we're going house to house to see family. My uncle Norman lives in Florida, so we aren't seeing his brother up north. Who else besides this Frances are we going to look up? He hasn't mentioned any friends still there."

"Her name is Phyllis. And you know it."

She gave a shrug. "I know. But I don't see what the big deal is about her. Why does he want to risk everything to go see her?"

"Haven't you ever wondered what happened to your high school sweetheart?"

"Nope. I didn't have a serious boyfriend in high school or college. I focused on my studies instead."

He could see that about her. "Of course you did."

"What is that supposed to mean?"

He held up his hands as if to surrender. "You're the serious type, Cecily, so you would naturally shun wasting time dating boys and focus instead on graduating with top honors."

"You make me sound like a fuddy-duddy."

"Am I wrong?"

"I said that I didn't have a serious boyfriend, not that I didn't date. I dated enough."

"Let me guess. Your ex was your first love."

She blinked several times, then abruptly walked away from him. He chased after her with the cart to the produce department. "Really? That jerk Tom was your first serious boyfriend?"

She shrugged and chose a bag of apples, then put them back and walked toward the peaches. She ripped off a plastic bag from the roll and placed several fruit inside. "Do you like peaches? These are a pretty good price."

"Sure. And we should get some grapes too."

"Good idea."

As she examined the display of red grapes, she sighed. "Yes, Tom was my first love. My only love."

"Only one, so far. You're still young enough to find another."

She turned and peered at him. "And is it so wrong to marry my first love?"

"No. I married mine."

Her mouth fell open, and she stared at him for a moment before asking, "Your first wife was your first love?"

"And my high school sweetheart." He looked at the reactions playing over her face. "Surprised?"

"Shocked. I figured you for a player."

"Based on what information?"

"Well, you have been married twice." She tied up the bag with the peaches and eyed a wide bin of watermelons. "Things my grandfather has shared about your conversations." She turned back and looked at the grocery cart. "I think we're good on snacks. What do you think?"

He thought he was going to have to talk to Burt about what information he shared with Cecily. But he gave her a smile. "All good."

At the cash register, Gus brought out his wallet, but Cecily had already handed over her credit card. He put a hand to stop the cashier from swiping it. "Wait. I'm paying for this."

"Don't worry about it. I've got it."

"I can pay for our snacks. I'm not destitute."

"I didn't say you were." Cecily whispered, "But I figured that since you're not working…"

"Who said I wasn't working?"

"You said you quit being a paramedic because you had burned out."

"That doesn't mean I don't work. I set my own hours, and I pay my own bills."

Cecily still didn't seem convinced.

"I make deliveries for Big Tony's Pizzeria on the weekends, and during the week I stock shelves and deliver groceries for Oakridge Market. A lot of seniors like to shop there. When I need extra money, I've been known to take on a few handyman jobs around the neighborhood."

"Okay, okay. Fine."

The cashier looked at them both then asked, "So who is paying for this?"

Gus handed her several bills, and Cecily took back her card. Once the groceries had been put in bags and placed in the cart, they walked in silence to his SUV. With the bags now in the trunk, Gus took the cart to the corral and returned to the car. Cecily stared at the cart corral. "What did you just do?"

"I put the cart back where it belongs."

"No, not where it belongs. You put it in the wrong slot. It says large carts, and ours was a small one."

"What?"

She walked to the corral and removed the cart he'd placed inside to position it under the correct sign. Back at the SUV, she said, "And people wonder what has happened to our society."

"It was an honest mistake. I placed the cart in the wrong place, yet I'm somehow responsible for the breakdown of the world?"

"We all have a responsibility toward one another, and that means following rules and expectations in order to make a better place for everyone." He couldn't help rolling his eyes. She pointed her finger at him. "That right there. You hold it all in disdain."

"Why are you are blowing this out of proportion?"

When he kept looking at her, she nodded. "I am, aren't I? Sorry. But disregarding the rules is a hot button for me."

"Then this trip should be interesting. Because my goal is to make sure your grandfather does all he wants to do whether it's okay with you or not."

"And my focus is to protect him. Even if that means protecting him from you."

"I'm not going to hurt him. Only encourage him to do more."

"Then I guess we're going to be at odds."

"Guess so." He got into his SUV and started the car.

GUS GROANED AND shielded his eyes from the sun, which had risen less than an hour before. "Tell me again why we need to get on the road this early."

Cecily put another tank into the back of his SUV, then frowned at him. "The sooner we get going, the sooner we can get back."

"I didn't know we were on a schedule."

"Pops has an important appointment with a new doctor in two weeks, so yes, we are." She turned to peer into the SUV. "Five tanks. Think it's enough?"

"He'll have the portable one that we can recharge. Those larger tanks are for emergencies only."

She sighed and looked over at Burt's

house. "I'd feel better if we could get another couple into your car, though."

"We probably won't even need one of them."

"But what if we get stranded and run out? Pops will be gasping for air and there won't be anything we can do for him."

"You really dwell on those worst-case scenarios, don't you?" He recalled their conversation the day before. She was doing what she could to protect Burt. He got that. "Five will be more than enough. Besides, we still need room for our luggage and any other things you think necessary to bring along."

Cecily looked unamused by his observations. Finally, she shrugged. "Fine. We can always go to a medical supply store to get more if we have to. They have one, I checked."

She stalked away to get more of…something she must think was necessary. She had already brought a large red-and-white striped duffel bag full of medicine and medical supplies. Plus, a smaller turquoise blue tote with the snacks they had bought the day before. And, two suitcases of hers and Burt's clothing and toiletries. He didn't know what else she could possibly think they needed to pack into the SUV.

To her retreating back, he called, "Leave the kitchen sink."

She gave a wave, then entered Burt's house next door. Another car pulled up to the curb, and Cecily's mom stepped out.

"Oh, good. You haven't left yet. I was afraid that I was going to miss you." Anna produced a couple of bulging plastic bags and crossed the lawn to hand them to him. "I bought you some snacks for your trip."

"I think your daughter has us covered."

"A few extras never hurt. Also, I baked banana muffins."

He thanked her and tried to find a place to put them that wouldn't get them smushed or crammed.

Cecily appeared with Pops, who had the portable air compressor strapped across his back like a backpack. He smiled at the sight of them. "Anna, I didn't know you were seeing us off."

She gave him a hug, then squeezed his chin. "I wouldn't miss this for the world."

She gave Cecily a hug. "Are you sure you have everything?"

"I hope so."

Gus stepped closer. "Anything you forgot, we can pick up on the way."

Anna nodded at him, then gave him a hug too. An awkward one-armed hug that lasted for a few seconds before she backed up. "Take care of them. You're carrying precious cargo in that SUV of yours."

"I know." He patted her back, wanting to reassure her.

"I'll call you from the Mackinac Bridge when we stop for lunch."

Cecily's mom looked at her. "You think you'll be there by then?"

"According to my research and timetables, we should be there no later than one p.m. And we will be halfway across the Upper Peninsula by the time we stop tonight, and to Lighthouse Bay by tomorrow afternoon."

Pops cleared his throat. "We'll see."

Cecily hugged her mom one more time. "I'll call you every night regardless of where we are."

"Please do."

They settled Burt in the front passenger seat, and Cecily took the back seat. She leaned out the window, waving to her mother as they pulled out of the driveway and onto the street. "See you next week."

Gus glanced at Cecily in the rearview mirror. She didn't seem happy that they had finally left. In fact, it looked like she was even more anxious than before. He hit the button for the radio to start and found an oldies station. The deejays played a trivia game against a caller. "I figured we'd stop for breakfast once we got past Flint. So in about an hour or so."

Cecily nodded but didn't meet his gaze in the mirror. Instead, she looked out the side window. Burt seemed pale in the seat beside him, but he also nodded. "I'll be ready for pancakes by then."

"If it's pancakes you want, it's pancakes you'll get."

The deejay's trivia contest segued to a string of hits that had topped the charts back in the years before Gus had been born, but he remembered hearing his parents play them on cassettes and eventually CDs.

Talk was minimal between the three of them, and Gus wondered if that's how the rest of the trip would play out. If so, it was going to be a long and boring one. To liven the mood a little, Gus asked, "So Burt, what are you most looking forward to seeing when we get to your hometown?"

"The old house. I'm hoping the current residents might let us get a tour of it. I wonder how much it has changed."

"It's been sixty years, so I'm sure it has changed quite a bit," Cecily added from the back seat. "They might have added on to it. Completely renovated the interior."

"Still, I'd like to see it one last time."

Gus snuck a peek at Cecily in the mirror. "What about you, Cecily? What are you looking forward to seeing?"

"The lighthouse the town is named for. It's supposed to still be working, so that would be something to see."

Burt turned to Gus. "What about you?"

"I want to put my feet in Lake Superior. It's the only one of the Great Lakes that I haven't been in. And I wouldn't mind seeing a waterfall or two."

"That sounds good to me too." Cecily caught his eye, and he gave her a wink.

BY THE TIME they stopped for breakfast, Cec was more than ready for a break. She felt as if she'd been crammed in the back seat for a lifetime. She needed to stretch her legs and visit the restroom, and a huge cup of coffee with lots of cream and sugar sounded amazing. They walked into the restaurant and were seated at a table near the back. Cec excused herself as soon as she ordered coffee.

In the bathroom, she examined the bags under her eyes. She had hardly slept last night. Instead, she'd tossed and turned, going over all the different ways this trip could go wrong. And then coming up with solutions for each possible problem. She'd woken up more tired than she'd been when she went to bed.

Her conversation with Gus the day before had left her unsettled. He was determined to let Pops do whatever he wanted on this trip. But there were things that weren't possible physically or emotionally. She only hoped she wouldn't have to be the spoilsport. That they could find some middle ground between Gus's penchant for risks and hers for caution.

When she returned to the table, a cup of coffee waited next to the menu at her place. She took a seat and looked over at Pops, who had his focus on the small sign on the table that advertised the specials for the day. "Blueberry pancakes, my favorite. But they probably won't be as good as your grandmother's. That woman could make angels weep with how good her pancakes were. Light. Airy. Perfection."

Cec gave him a smile and turned back to her perusal of the menu. She didn't remember her grandmother's cooking as fondly as Pops did. She recalled the blueberry pancakes being closer to hockey pucks than light and airy, but she wasn't going to contradict his memory. His love for her grandmother clearly colored his feelings for her cooking. Though Granny's pot roast had been the best she'd ever eaten. He was right about that one.

The server arrived at their table, refilling coffee cups, and they put in their orders. Cecily brought out her notebook and marked off their location and mileage. They were making good time and should definitely make it to the Mackinac Bridge by lunchtime.

Pops cleared his throat, which led to a coughing fit. Cec reached over to check the portable condenser. "It's fine," he said in what sounded more like a croak. Once he had the coughing under control, he looked at the two of them. "There's actually something I'd like to talk to you both about."

Cec turned to Gus, who gave a shrug. "What's on your mind, Burt?" he asked.

"I'd like to take a detour before we get to Mackinac."

"A detour where?" Cec glanced at her journal. They didn't have room for extra stops in the time line.

"I'd like to visit the old college campus once more. It's only about an hour and a half from here. I thought we could tour the campus. Have lunch. Then get back on the road to Mackinac this afternoon."

Cec turned again to Gus, who was their designated driver for the trip since it was his SUV they were using. "What do you think?"

Gus looked at Pops. "Any reason for the sudden nostalgia for your old alma mater?"

"I guess I was thinking about all the places that made me, and that's one of the big ones. It's where I earned my degree. Met my wife. And started on the road that led to where I am now." Pops smiled at them, and Cec didn't see how she could refuse him. At least not this soon into their trip.

She nodded. "If Gus is okay with it, I don't see why we couldn't stop."

"That's what I hoped you'd say."

"But that doesn't mean I'm going to let you hijack all my carefully laid plans." She waggled a finger at him, but her words lacked fire.

"Maybe we could find the professor's house where I met your grandmother. Wouldn't that be something?"

POPS SHOOK HIS head as they drove down another side street. "None of these look familiar. And I'm sure it was on Cypress." He frowned. "Or was it Sycamore? Maybe Birch. Anyways, it was a tree of some sort."

Cec caught Gus looking at her in the rearview mirror. They seemed to be laughing, which was a good sign since she was ready to give up on this search Pops had insisted upon. "We've driven down all the streets next to the campus."

"Not all of them, since I didn't find the house, did I?" Pops sounded angry. "This just doesn't look familiar at all."

"It's been a long time."

"You don't need to remind me how long it's been. I know how long it's been." Pops harrumphed and stared out the passenger window.

"Burt, why don't we go take a walk on campus? Maybe if we look again after, you'll be able to see it with fresh eyes."

"I'm telling you, it's on a street named after a tree. It was a gray house with a large front porch that wrapped around it. I kissed your grandmother for the first time on that porch. Just a quick peck before her father came looking to find out why she took so long to come inside." He sighed. "It had a porch swing where I'd sit with her in the evenings, and we'd dream about our future together."

"Sounds nice."

She smiled at Pops. "Why don't we go

back and take that other street? Maybe it was on the other section of campus." Pops frowned and turned, trying to figure out where they should go next.

"Sure."

Gus was so sweet to be so accommodating to Pops. He didn't argue or grumble but slowed down when necessary to give Pops enough time to get his bearings. It was like Cec was seeing him through a different lens. Not the cantankerous, nosy neighbor, but the good friend. Good man. Maybe he'd meant it when he said he would do everything to make sure Pops accomplished what he needed to on this road trip.

She stared out the window just then. Gray house. Big wraparound porch. But no porch swing. "Hey, Pops. What about this house on our right?"

Pops squinted. "No, that's more of a greenish gray. The house was a blue gray."

"It could have faded with time or even changed color completely." Or his memory could be flawed. Cec often wondered how accurate his memory was after all this time.

Gus pulled to the curb and let the engine

idle. "Maybe if you got out and looked at it a little closer, it might jog your memory."

Pops unplugged the portable air condenser and slipped it over one shoulder as he stepped out of the SUV and walked up the sidewalk toward the house, Cec following close behind him in case his balance was off. They returned a moment later, Pops shaking his head. "It's close, but I'm not sure." He got into the car and Cec shut the door for him. "I'm tired of looking for something that could be long gone. Let's just go to the campus."

The north end of campus housed the buildings that Pops remembered from his tenure at the college, but he seemed to enjoy seeing the newer buildings too. "I don't think I could have made it on time to all my classes if I had to go from one end to the other in fifteen minutes like I used to. At least not on foot."

Because it was summer, fewer classes were in session, so many of the buildings had been closed for the break. However, Pops did find an open door into one of the older buildings. He whistled as they walked down the empty hallways. "It's the same, but different. If I close my eyes, I can hear Professor Trimble lecturing on Shakespeare's tragedies and Professor Voss talking about classroom management." He took a deep breath through his nose, which caused him to cough. When he caught his breath, he smiled. "Still smells the same. Though I think they must be painting one of the classrooms. Seems like they were always doing that when I was here."

He turned to them both and rubbed his hands. "Who's hungry for lunch? I'm buying."

CHAPTER SIX

AN HOUR AFTER they got back on to the road, Burt had fallen asleep in the passenger seat, and from the looks of it, Cecily wasn't that far behind. Gus watched her in the rearview mirror as she blinked her eyes, yawning and stretching in the seat.

"Go ahead. Take a nap," he told her. "I'm fine driving."

She shook her head. "I don't want to sleep now and then not be able to sleep tonight." She yawned once more, then shuddered. "I didn't get much sleep last night, but I'll be fine."

"You'd be better with a quick nap."

"No, it's fine."

Gus gazed at the long road in front of them. "There's a rest stop coming up. Anyone need it?"

Burt moved in the seat beside him, then raised a finger. "I wouldn't object to stopping."

"I thought you were asleep, Pops."

"Just resting my eyes for a few minutes." He blinked several times, then turned to Cecily. "I know you brought the snack bag. I wouldn't mind having something."

"We just had lunch."

"I could use something a little sweet, and I know you packed those cookies I love."

When the exit for the rest area came up, Gus eased off the freeway and found a parking spot close to the restrooms. He turned off the engine and rolled down the windows. "Wait a moment, and I'll help you to the restroom."

"I'm fine. I don't need your help."

"Pops…"

Burt growled. "I said I'm fine. Stop treating me like a child."

Gus held up his hands in surrender, and Burt slid out of the SUV and headed inside the building. Gus turned to look at Cecily. "Now or never."

She shook her head. "I'm fine." She unbuckled her seatbelt and leaned over the back of the seat to peer in the back. "I'll find those cookies for Pops." She pulled out a turquoise bag and placed it on the seat next to her before rummaging through the contents and finally pulling out the package of chocolate sandwich crème cookies. "Got them."

Gus looked out the passenger window and pointed to a picnic table under a group of trees. "Why don't we go eat our snacks over there? Get some fresh air."

"We can eat in the car while we keep driving."

"Why are you so worried about sticking to your imaginary schedule?"

"First of all, it's not imaginary." She lifted a clipboard from beneath the snack bag. "It's all written down so that we take full advantage of our trip but still get back in time for Pops's next medical appointment. And second, Pops already hijacked the schedule with the unplanned stop to the college."

"Exactly. The schedule is already out the window. Let it go."

"Just because you don't like being confined by something as mundane as a schedule—"

"I don't mind it. I just prefer to live a little looser." He got out of the SUV, then popped his head back inside. "It will take maybe an extra fifteen minutes to sit and relax. Half hour, tops. I can make up most of that on the freeway."

Cecily eyed him. "Fine. I'm sure Pops would appreciate sitting out for a moment before we have to get back on the road. But it's fifteen minutes, not thirty, then we go."

Gus gave her a salute, then walked to the picnic table. A second later, Cecily joined him. She placed the turquoise bag on the table, then shielded her eyes with her hand as she looked over at the restroom. "I haven't seen Pops come out yet. Have you?"

"Give the old guy a chance. I'm sure he's fine. Besides, the way he practically bit my head off earlier, I don't want to give him any more reason to snap at me."

"What if something happened? Or what if he walked out and didn't see us? And then he panicked and had an attack or something, and he's trying to find us before he dies."

Gus looked at her intently. "Wow. You really worry about a lot of things that won't happen."

"It could happen."

"*There* you are." Burt joined them at the

table. "I walked out of the restroom, but you two weren't in the car. Luckily, I saw you sitting here."

Gus raised his brow as if to say he was right, she returned the gesture. "We thought it might be nice to take a little snack break."

Burt took a seat at the table, then accepted the opened package of cookies from Cecily. He took several and then passed the bag to Gus. "I do love these cookies."

"Which is why I bought them for the trip."

Gus waved off the cookies. "I'm more interested in something salty. Where are those barbecue chips?"

THEY REACHED THE MACKINAC BRIDGE and Cec longed to get out of the car and run around to get the muscles in her legs going again. They ached with disuse, and this was only the first day of their trip.

Gus edged into traffic to cross the bridge, his hands gripping the steering wheel, the knuckles white with effort. There was no wind today to buffer the SUV, but he seemed nervous as they approached the upward slope. The suspension bridge was five miles, but it might as well have been twenty-five as it stretched ahead of them.

"It's okay," she said softly.

Pops stirred in the front seat and turned to look at her. "Nervous about the crossing, are you?" She replied with a shake of her head, but her stomach tightened at his words. Her grandfather reached over and patted her hand, which clung to the back of his seat. "We'll be fine. Mighty Mac will hold us up," he said.

"*I* know that," Gus answered from the driver's seat. But his jaw clenched, and his eyebrows furrowed.

Cec winced as some of the suspension cables clanged and swayed. "I'll still feel better once we're safely on the other side."

Pops chuckled. "I never took the two of you to be such nervous Normans."

Gus turned toward Pops, then quickly jerked his head back to focus on the road. "Don't you mean nervous Nellies?"

"I say Norman because my brother Norman had what you would call a weak stomach for things. A test. A fire drill. The possibility of a thunderstorm. They'd all throw him into a tizzy." Pops grinned.

"Yep, I'd say I've got two Normans in the car with me."

Cec tried to imagine her grandfather as a young boy. "And what? You were the fearless one?"

Pops shrugged. "I wouldn't say fearless, but I was the one more likely to put on a brave front and take a chance."

There was a bump in the road, and the SUV jumped slightly, causing Cec to reach out and brace herself against the seat and the door. "What was that?"

"Just a pothole."

Gus confirmed. "Yeah. Just a huge chunk of the road missing that could shred my tires." He groaned and glanced at Cec through the rearview mirror. "Now I'm the one making dire predictions."

"I never predicted this." She closed her eyes and took a deep breath. "How much more do we have to go?"

"Almost there," Gus answered, and she opened her eyes to see that they were starting the descent.

She let out a sigh of relief even though they hadn't yet reached the other side. Still, they were close enough. "Maybe we can take the ferry over on the way home."

Gus nodded. "I like the sound of that."

Pops chuckled more. "And miss the fun of this again?"

"Yes," Gus and Cec replied simultaneously.

When they had reached the end of the bridge, a sign welcomed them to the Upper Peninsula. Another sign pointed them to Bridge View Park, and Gus followed the arrows to pull into the parking lot beside it. As soon as the car stopped, he got out and put his hands on the outer car frame and stared at the pavement. Cec leaned toward Pops and asked, "Do you think he's okay?"

"Let's just give him a moment." Pops turned to her. "I know your plan had us getting farther north, but I'm tuckered out. I think we should stop for the night here in St. Ignace."

"Pops..."

"I'm sorry, baby girl. This body of mine feels like it needs to sleep."

It seemed like that's most of what he'd done on the ride, but she didn't want to argue. She reminded herself that Pops was in charge of their road trip, so if he said they would stay the night here, then it was her job to find an available motel. She pulled out her cell phone and started to search.

After the fifth call, she hung up and gave a soft groan. Gus, who had rejoined them in the car, looked at her. "Something wrong?"

"No room there either. I guess with the Fourth of July coming up, this is one of the city's busiest tourist seasons, and hotels are all booked with reservations. I can't get two rooms anywhere."

Pops sighed. "I think we're all adults, so if we were to get one room—"

"Pops!"

"With two beds. Gus and I can share one, and you'll get the other." Pops looked at her. "I think that's our best option."

"No, our best option is to keep driving to the place where I already made the reservation for tonight."

"Which is still at least two hours away." Gus said. "Burt is right. If we can get a room here, that's our best option." He looked at Pops. "But if we can't, we'll drive to the next town."

Cec looked at her phone. "Fine. I'll make

some more calls. And if we can't get two rooms, I'll see if they have one with two beds."

After three more calls, she was able to locate a room with two queen beds at a motel on the outskirts of town. It didn't sit well with her to stop so soon for the night, but she gave her credit card number over the phone to reserve the room. She ended the call and looked at the two men. "It's more inland than the touristy places, but we're not here to be sightseers."

"Right." Gus put the keys in the ignition and the engine roared to life. "Let's go check this place out."

GUS PARKED THE SUV to the right of the open stairwell that led to the second floor. Cecily frowned from the back seat. "I should have asked if it was a first-floor room when I booked it."

Burt looked out the windshield to the stairs. "I can make it just fine. Slower than I used to maybe, but just fine all the same." He unplugged the portable air condenser from the dashboard and stepped out of the SUV before pulling the strap over one shoulder. "I'll take Twain here with me and meet the two of you up there."

He started the climb, and Gus watched the older man before turning to Cecily. "I'll grab the suitcases. If you want to go up with him to make sure he's okay."

She nodded, then reached into the back seat to grab her purse and the red-and-white tote bag that contained medical supplies they might need.

She left Gus as he opened the back of the SUV and pulled out his suitcase and one of the two that Cecily had brought. He'd have to come down for the other on a second trip. He looked at the stairwell to find that Burt had made it to the first landing but still had a short flight to go. *Come on, Burt. You can make it.*

When Burt made it up to the second floor, Gus picked up the suitcases and took the stairs. Entering the motel room, he spotted Burt sitting on the bed, gasping for air as Cecily searched the medical bag. She plucked out the prefilled morphine shots in a plastic bag and readied one. "Here, Pops. Open your mouth. This will make you feel better."

"I…don't need…it."

Gus put the suitcases by the front window and crossed the room to squat down next to Pops. "She's right, Burt. You don't want to get worse, do you?"

"I'll…be…fine."

"You promised you'd listen to me, Pops. So, stop being stubborn and take your medicine."

Burt opened his mouth, and she depressed the plunger so that the morphine dispensed into his mouth. "Thank you." She turned her back on Pops and walked to the sink beside a door that probably led to the bathroom. She rinsed the syringe and plunger, then laid them on the counter on a clean white towel.

Gus kept an eye on Burt. "Why don't you take a quick nap while I finish unpacking the car?"

Cecily turned from the sink. "Could you bring up the snack bag with you when you come back? And I think we should bring dinner in tonight."

"There's…no need," Burt said.

Cecily shot Gus a look, which he understood to mean that she wasn't going to listen to Burt's protests. "The turquoise bag with the snacks."

"I remember." Gus glanced back at Burt. "Anything else you think we might need from the car?"

"That should do it."

He nodded and left the room.

Down at the SUV, he went searching for the snack bag. It wasn't in the back. And he didn't need to search the front seat to know it wasn't there. Where had it gone? He searched one more time, but it didn't bring any results. He sighed, then lifted the suitcase in one hand and the plastic bag from Anna in the other.

"I've got good news and bad news," he said as he entered the motel room.

Cecily turned from where she had been talking to Burt. She looked at the things in Gus's hands. "Where's the snack bag?"

"That's the bad news. We must have left it at the rest stop earlier."

Cecily groaned and tipped her head back. "I thought you grabbed it off the picnic table before we left."

"I thought you grabbed it."

"Well, I didn't."

"I didn't either." Gus placed the suitcase next to the others. "It doesn't matter who didn't grab the bag. The fact is that one lucky family is now the happy owners of Burt's favorite cookies. And my favorite chips."

"Is that the good news?" Cecily asked.

"For them, sure. But the good news for us is we still have Anna's banana muffins. And I also saw that there's a convenience store right across the parking lot to replace those snacks. And it's right next door to a sandwich place and a burger joint. So, we have plenty of options for dinner."

CEC PEERED AT the shelves in the convenience store. The loss of the snack bag was a minor one, yet it still rankled. She should have checked before they left the rest area, but she'd been helping Pops get back to the SUV and assumed that Gus would grab it. She picked up a package of Pop's favorite cookies and moved to the next aisle that held the potato chips, where she found Gus standing and contemplating the different choices. "They don't have your favorite?"

He turned to look at her, shaking his head, and choosing a bag of plain potato chips. "That's okay. We can look for them when we get up to Lighthouse Bay tomorrow. I'll live."

They went to the cooler and picked out a few drinks to take back to the room to go with the burgers they'd ordered from the place next door. They were headed to the cash register when Cec thought of something else they'd need. She told Gus to start checking out and headed to an aisle that contained paper products, choosing a small pack of paper plates and another of napkins. She knew they could have made do, but she didn't want to completely rough it.

She met Gus at the register and placed the plates and napkins on the counter. "You do prepare for every possibility, don't you?"

"Why don't you do it more?"

"A lot of times I had to react in the moment because there wasn't time to prepare. I guess that's what made me a good medic and later a paramedic. I could react calmly in a crisis and use what I had on hand to make it work." He pulled out his wallet as the cashier announced their total.

Cec waved his wallet away. "I've got it this time."

"You paid for the room. I can buy the snacks."

She pulled an envelope from her purse. "My mom gave me this before we left in case we had an emergency." She looked at the cashier. "I'd say this qualifies."

"It could be worse, so you save that for later just in case." He pulled out a few bills and handed them to the cashier.

Cec conceded but insisted that she'd pay for their sandwiches. They took their purchases, now in plastic bags, and walked next door to the deli. Their order wasn't quite ready, so they stood near the door, waiting to hear her name called.

Cec glanced out the front window at the motel across the parking lot. The light shone in their room where she knew Pops lay on the bed, waiting for their return. She'd debated whether they should leave him alone, but he'd insisted he'd be fine for the short time it would take for them to pick up dinner. Reluctantly, she'd agreed. "Do you think he's going to be okay?"

Gus looked at her and nodded. "He's a tough guy. He's just tired. So, we'll let him sleep and get back on the road tomorrow."

"Those stairs nearly killed him. I should have checked. This is all my fault."

"His house is all one floor, so you couldn't have known he'd react like that. But we'll be sure to find a place that's on the main floor from here on out." Gus shifted his weight and put the plastic bag he carried in the other hand. "You're taking good care of him, Cecily. Stop beating yourself up."

Her shoulders slumped. "I don't know what I'm doing here, period."

"You're doing the best you can. That means a lot. Burt's always saying how great you are at caring for him."

"But it still doesn't feel like it's enough."

Gus looked at her, and put his free hand on her bare shoulder, sending tingles up her spine. "You're doing fine."

She shook her head. "You don't need to be condescending."

"How was that condescending? I said you're doing fine."

"It's more the way you said it." She knew she was taking offense where none was being given, and yet it irritated her like sand in a sensitive spot. "My mom is the nurse, not me. But she's been working long hours and hasn't been able to step in like she wants to. And after the divorce, I needed a place to stay and Pops needed help, so it seemed the perfect solution for the both of us. And if I'm muddling around, then you should at least extend me some grace and compassion."

Gus blinked at her. "Are you finished?"

She could have gone on, but she gave a short nod. Finished for now, at least.

"Then I'll just say that you're right. I should have been more understanding… But you and Burt have both learned how to do better. And it may sound harsh but your penchant for preparing for any situation will help as we get closer to his death."

She glanced out at the motel room window. Five months since Pops's diagnosis, and she was no closer to being able to say that *d* word. "Hopefully that won't be for a long, long time."

"Cecily…" She turned back to look at Gus. He opened his mouth, then shook his head. "Hopefully a very long time."

"But you don't think it will be?"

He stared at her long and hard, his eyes

growing misty until the host called her name to let them know their dinner was ready.

GUS FINISHED OFF the last crust of his Reuben sandwich from the paper plate. When he'd pictured having dinner that evening, he hadn't imagined sitting on a bed next to Burt, his back propped up against a headboard watching game shows on television in a motel room. He glanced over at Cecily, who had her back to them while she talked on the phone to her mom. He knew for sure she hadn't pictured their trip starting this way either.

Cecily ended the call then turned back to them, picked up the remote, and increased the volume. "Mom says hi," she said.

Burt glanced over to her. "Doesn't sound like she was surprised we didn't get as far as you'd planned."

Cecily made a face, then plugged her cell phone charger into the outlet by the nightstand between the two beds. "It's as if she knows something that we don't. And it can't be a mother's intuition either."

"And why not?" Burt asked.

"Because I'm too old to be mothered like that."

Now Burt made a face and turned to look at Gus. "Do you hear this girl? Too old to need a mother? I need a mother now and then, even at my age."

"I didn't say I didn't need her. Just that I don't need her looking out for me like that. I can take care of myself."

Burt made a noise, and Gus grinned at that. When Cecily glared at Gus, he shrugged. "I'm not saying you can't. Far be it from me to doubt your abilities. But Burt is right. Every once in a while, I wish that my mom was around to look after me."

"What would you need a mother for right now?"

"I could use some advice on what I should be doing next. Do I stay in Thora and look for a job there or pull up stakes again and move on? Should I be looking in the medical field or have I burnt myself out to the point I need something completely fresh? Is now the time to be searching or is it better to wait?"

Cecily had a confused expression. "To wait for what?"

Gus glanced at Burt, who gave him a wary look. He shrugged again. "That's my point." He then stood and grabbed his cell phone from his back pocket. "In fact, you've reminded me that it's long past time I called and talked to my mom."

Before he left, he picked up the empty foam boxes from their dinners. "I'll take these to the trash during my walk."

"You're going for a walk right now?"

Gus gave Cecily a smile. "Yes, Mom. It's still light out, but I'll be sure to be home by the time it's dark." He turned and winked at Burt, who chuckled.

After he left the room, he took the stairs to the first floor then crossed to the large dumpster at the edge of the parking lot. He lifted the heavy lid and tossed in the boxes. He'd used the excuse of calling his mom to get out of the motel room, and now that he'd left, he realized this wasn't the right time to call her. She lived in Washington state with his stepdad, and with the time difference, she wouldn't be home from her job at the bookstore yet.

Still, he longed to hear her voice, so he called her cell phone and wasn't surprised when the call got directed to her voicemail. He listened to her message and waited for the beep. "Hey, Mom. I know you're working, but I thought I'd call and let you know I was thinking of you. I'm on a road trip to Michigan's Upper Peninsula. Can't wait to see the sights. Miss you and Roy. Love you."

He hung up the phone and returned it to his back pocket. Calling her had made him miss her all the more, but he didn't need to talk to her to know what her advice would be right now. Don't rush into anything you might regret. It had been her warning to him before both of his marriages. And she'd been right every time. But now?

He already knew he wasn't rushing to get back to work as a paramedic. He had his fill of life, death and everything in between in the last four years. But if he didn't return to that, what would he do? What did he want to do? He'd been in the field since he was eighteen, more than half of his life.

He started walking back to the motel but turned toward the street instead of the stairs when he got there. After being in the car all day, his legs wanted to keep moving.

He stayed on the sidewalk but peered at the different business fronts as he walked by. A cell phone store. A bakery. A dry cleaner and laundromat. Another convenience store. When he reached the end of the block, he crossed the street and walked down the other side. More stores and restaurants passed. All of them aimed at attracting tourist dollars. A small two-screen movie theater sat back from the street, its sign offering big budget films and fresh, hot popcorn.

By the time he'd made it to the end of the block and crossed the street again, he felt ready to go back to the room.

The walk hadn't revealed many answers, but he knew why he wasn't ready to move on from Thora just yet. Time was running out with Burt, and Gus didn't want to miss any of it.

When Gus opened the motel room door, he saw that Burt had fallen asleep. The light by their bed had been turned off, probably by Cecily, who lay on the other bed, remote in hand, flipping channels on the television. She looked up at him. "How's your mom?"

"At work, so I got her voicemail."

"Oh. You were gone for a while, so I figured you had gotten a hold of her."

"I walked down the street for a bit. Found a bakery that might work for breakfast tomorrow before we get back on the road." He took a seat on the edge of her bed, and she shifted her feet to make space for him. He glanced over at Burt. "How's he doing?"

She shrugged and laid the remote on the bed. "Worn out. He didn't seem to eat much tonight."

"He didn't eat much today period. Picked at his meals."

"I'm worried."

"Cecily…"

"I'm not saying we shouldn't have come on this trip, but you have to admit this is not the best way to start out."

"It's not the best, but this is what he wants."

"I know." She looked down at her hands. "I know. But it's still upsetting."

Gus reached out and placed one hand over hers. "Worrying doesn't help him. Or you, Cecily. When it's his time, none of the worrying will bring him back."

She got off the bed and stood before him.

"I'm going to change into my pajamas. Do you need to get in the bathroom before I do?"

"It's okay to talk about his death. Burt and I discuss it all the time."

She moved past him as if she couldn't get away from him fast enough. She grabbed a stack of clothes from the top of the dresser and sprinted to the door that led to the toilet and bathtub. "I'll be out in a minute then."

"Cecily…"

But she had already barricaded herself in the bathroom and shut the door.

CEC TOOK HER time putting on her pajamas, a tank top and boxers with kittens printed all over them. She looked down at herself and wondered if maybe she should have packed something that covered her up more. But then, she hadn't planned on sharing a motel room with Gus.

Before she opened the bathroom door, she pressed her forehead against it, steeling herself for the conversation that Gus seemed to be determined to have. Didn't he understand she couldn't think beyond what would happen with Pops that day?

She couldn't be wondering about life after he was gone. Couldn't talk about his...

She took a deep breath, then walked out of the bathroom. Gus seemed to have found an old black-and-white Western on one of the television channels. He glanced at her from his side of the bed. "Feel better?" he asked.

She nodded and walked briskly to her bed and pulled the covers aside to get in.

Gus turned down the volume. "It's still early, but I can turn off the television if you want me to so you can sleep."

"It's fine. I thought I'd read for a little while before I go to sleep."

"If you need me to turn it off, just say the word."

"Okay."

The book she'd bought for the road trip rested on the nightstand, so she retrieved it and opened it to the first chapter. She hadn't finished the first page when she sighed and placed it beside her. "I don't like talking about...you know."

"You mean death."

"Right."

Cec glanced over at Burt, who snored

softly on the side of the bed closest to her. He looked peaceful.

Gus kept silent from his side of the bed. Was he hoping she'd say more?

"I just keep wishing that he'll get better. That we'll have more time."

She knew it sounded childish to be wishing for something that was impossible. But if anyone deserved a miracle, it was Burt. He'd lost his only son to cancer and then his wife to the same disease years later. And now he had to face it himself? "It's just not fair."

She blinked at the tears that she was trying to hold back. Burt might wake up, and she'd hate for him to see her crying. She was so careful to hide her tears from him, waiting until she was alone. She had to be strong for him. Had to show him a brave front because he was doing that for her too.

Gus looked at her from over Pops's sleeping form. "None of this is fair."

Well, at least he agreed with her on that. "And I will talk about...the end eventually. But not now."

Nothing was said for a moment, then Gus spoke up. "I just don't want it to be harder for you later on, if you don't know what he wants when it happens. It's important he has things the way he wants them, right?" Burt snorted a little in his sleep and Gus lowered his voice to a whisper. "While he's still able to make decisions."

"Seems like he made all those decisions already."

"What about—"

"Gus, stop. Please." She sat up and glanced at Pops. "Not in front of him."

"He has to be involved in this discussion."

"Then we'll talk about it later when he's awake. Much later. So good night." She grabbed her book and turned away from the pair of them, and instead faced the door and front window with the curtain drawn. She opened her book and tried to concentrate on the words.

"Good night, Cecily. We'll get an early start tomorrow."

She heard Gus shut off the television and settle into the bed. She promised herself she'd go to sleep after the first chapter.

FAINT SUNLIGHT PEEKED in from the edges of the drawn curtain. Even with the sun starting to rise, it still had to be early, right? After all, Cec had set the alarm on her cell phone for six thirty, and it hadn't chimed. She rolled onto her back and stared at the ceiling. If her alarm hadn't woken her up, what had?

A soft snuffle from the other bed reminded her that her companions' snoring and the white noise from the oxygen condenser had kept her awake most of the night. Then a high-pitched beep sounded. That was the noise that had awakened her. The condenser's alarm was going off.

She scrambled out of the bed to peer at the condenser that lay next to Pops's side of the bed. Dead battery. She followed the power cord from the condenser to where it should have been plugged into the wall beside the nightstand. How had it gotten unplugged during the middle of the night? She plugged in the cord, then watched as the battery charging light lit up.

Standing, she crouched over Pops. In the darkened room, she couldn't see very well, so she turned on the light closest to his bed and gasped when she saw him. His ashen face looked slack, and his lips had turned blue. She put her ear on his chest. A faint heartbeat. She straightened and raised her voice to ask, "Pops? Can you hear me?"

Gus bolted upright from the far side of the bed. "What happened?"

"The condenser got unplugged somehow, and the battery ran out. I don't know how long he's been lying here without oxygen. His heart is still beating, but very faint, and he's turning blue."

Gus bounded off the bed and grabbed a bag from his side of the floor. He pulled out a stethoscope and placed the metal against Pops's chest. Then he readjusted the cannula in his nose while calling his name. Pops stirred and slowly opened his eyes. "What's all…the…fuss? I'm…trying to…sleep."

"Can you take a few deep breaths for me? Breathe in through your nose like smelling a rose. Then blow out through your mouth like blowing out a candle." Gus mimicked the action.

"I know…how…to breathe… I've…been doing…it…longer…than you've…been alive."

Cec motioned to her phone on the nightstand. "Should we call 911? Maybe we need to get him to a hospital."

"Not yet." Gus checked Burt's heartbeat again. "We just need to get him to breathe low and slow. He'll be fine."

"I'm…fine. Stop…fussing…at me."

Cec sighed and wilted back onto her bed. Pops snapping at Gus meant he was going to be okay. She'd been on the receiving end of his crankiness enough to have figured that out. Gus looked over at her, then stood, wearing a T-shirt with Georgia Bulldogs imprinted on the front and light gray pajama shorts. His hair was a tousled mess. "What time is it?"

She felt her cheeks warm as she realized he'd caught her staring at his cute, disheveled state, and quickly averted her gaze. She distracted herself by grabbing her cell phone and reading the display. "It's not quite six yet."

"I'm going to run down to the car and get one of the bigger oxygen tanks."

She turned back to look at him. He had pulled on a pair of jogging pants and sat on the edge of the bed putting on his tennis shoes. "I already plugged in the condenser."

"The oxygen tank has a higher output of oxygen, so until his color improves, I'd feel better having him on a tank. Plus, it will give the portable machine time to recharge." He stood and searched the top of the dresser opposite the bed until he located and grabbed his keys. "We'll have to let the front desk know we'll be staying at least another day."

Cec glanced at Pops and nodded. "Probably best if we do."

Gus walked to the front door and opened it. Moments later, he returned with one of the oxygen tanks. He opened the gauges, then swapped out the cannula from the portable condenser to the one attached to the tank. Then he sat on the bed beside Pops, watching the older man breathe. His color still looked gray, and the lines around his eyes even more pronounced. He put his fingers on Pops's wrist to check his pulse.

"I should have checked the power cord before I turned off the light last night." Cec watched Gus count the heartbeats. "I always make sure his breathing tube is free

of kinks and that everything is working before I go to bed. But last night, I…"

Gus shook his head. "It's not your fault."

"But it is. I was the one who plugged the
machine in when we got settled last night.
I was the one who gave him his meds and
checked that he had what he needed. But I
didn't check the cord. He could have died."
She buried her head in her hands. One day
out on their road trip, and she'd come close
to killing Pops.

"It was…me…baby girl."

She opened her eyes to look at Pops. He
looked back at her. "I got…up to…go to
the…bathroom…and un-unplugged it."
He paused as he took several deep breaths
before continuing. "I forgot to…plug it
back…in."

"Oh, Pops."

He gave a half-hearted shrug. "I can't…
remember…so good…these…days."

"You scared me. I thought you were…"
*Don't think about that. Put it out of your
head. Don't think…* "But I should have
heard the alarm sooner and plugged it
back in. I'm closest to it, and I slept right
through it. Didn't even notice."

"It was…me… Silly mis-mistake."

"We can't afford to make stupid mistakes, Pops. I knew this road trip was a bad idea. Maybe we should cancel the rest of the trip. We can leave for home tomorrow and forget…"

"Cecily, stop."

Gus was only whispering her name, yet she felt the force of his words and realized that he'd been saying them for a while. But she'd been ignoring him. Pops looked defeated. He had been pale before, but this outburst from her seemed to have drained even more out of him. She winced and immediately regretted what she'd said.

"Burt knows what's at stake better than either one of us."

She blinked a few times, then nodded. Gus was right. It was a simple mistake, and it was no more Pops's fault than it was hers for not hearing the alarm. "I should probably shower and get dressed. Then we'll discuss what happens next."

ONCE GUS HEARD the shower running, he pulled a vial out of the medical bag and filled a syringe with the light pink–tinged fluid. Burt shook his head. "I don't need…it."

"Your color isn't back to what it should be. The morphine will help you breathe."

"I don't…like the…way it makes…me feel."

"Tough." Gus held out the syringe until Burt sighed and opened his mouth. Gus pressed the plunger in, then got off the bed to rinse it out.

"It makes…me sleepy."

"More rest is a good thing right now."

"Don't want…to sleep…the rest…of my life…away."

Gus turned and zipped up the medical bag. "I understand that, but right now you need to get your breathing better and sleep a bit more. It's early still. There's plenty of time to doze while I convince your granddaughter that we're not going home. At least, not this soon."

Burt chuckled until it made him start to cough. "Good…luck."

Gus grinned at him. "She is one determined woman when it comes to keeping you alive. She loves you very much." Burt nodded as he closed his eyes. Gus patted his arm over the bed covers. "You get some rest."

Gus watched Burt for a few moments, then got to his feet and glanced toward the closed bathroom door. Part of him admired the way Cecily took care of her grandfather, while the other, bigger part wished she'd back off just a little. Burt knew his limitations, for the most part, anyways. And the poor guy was not trying to hurry his death. If anything, he seemed to want to enjoy as much as he could out of the life he had left.

The water was off now, and Gus figured Cecily would be back in the room soon. So, he quickly grabbed the duffel bag he'd packed with his clothes and pulled out a clean T-shirt to wear with the shorts he'd worn the day before. A day sitting around the motel room would be casual and quiet, he assumed.

When Cecily emerged from the bathroom, her cheeks were still pink from the steam in the shower, and her long blond hair hung wet down her back, past her shoulder blades that peeked through the back of her tank top. She stopped short when she discovered him standing and staring at her. "What's wrong? How's Pops?"

"Nothing. He's sleeping."

She glanced at Burt, nodding. "He seems to be doing better."

"He is. I gave him some morphine to help with the breathing."

"Which is why I think we should go home tomorrow."

"Actually, it's why we should keep going to his hometown."

Cecily turned to him, her blue eyes icy and cold. "Why? So he can die there instead of at home, where he should have been this whole time?"

Gus took a deep breath and reminded himself that it was Cecily's fear that was currently talking. "He's never going to get another chance to do this. Time is running out, so we need to follow through. I know you want to protect him—"

"Of course I do. I'd surround him in bubble wrap if it would work."

"That might compromise his breathing more than it already is."

"You know what I mean."

He did. If he could do anything to ensure that Burt would have more good days ahead of him, he'd move heaven and earth. But his skills were as limited as Burt's time left with them. "This last trip is very important to him. We need to do everything we can to make sure he gets there."

The fight in Cecily's eyes seemed to cool, and her body relaxed. "I know you're right, but…" She closed her eyes. "I'm so scared of losing him."

Gus walked toward her and put an arm around her shoulder. "I am too."

Cecily leaned into him, putting the top of her head against his chest. Gus rubbed her back, then gave her a hug. "Why don't you stay here with Burt while I run down to that bakery and pick up breakfast? I don't know about you, but I could use an extra-large dose of caffeine right now."

She tipped her head back, her sad eyes meeting his. "Double cream, double sugar for me."

CHAPTER SEVEN

THERE WERE ONLY so many talk shows that a person could take. Cec collapsed onto the stack of pillows on her bed and searched for the remote control amid the blankets and comforter. Pops held it up from his bed. "Looking for this?"

"Please change the channel. I can't take any more paternity test results."

"Your grandmother loved these shows. They were one of her only guilty pleasures." He did turn the volume down on the television. "Why don't you and Gus take a walk around town or something once he gets back from the front office? Your legs could probably use some stretching."

"I'm fine."

"I didn't ask if you were fine. I said you need to get out of this room for a little bit."

"I'm not leaving you by yourself today, so no thank you. I'm fine right here."

"I'm too old for a babysitter."

The door to the room opened, and Gus entered. "We're fine to stay here for tonight, but they are booked solid for the rest of the week. I keep forgetting the Fourth of July holiday is coming up."

"While you were gone, I called the motel where we're staying up north to let them know we'll be arriving a day later. It's all set. And they confirmed that our rooms are on the first floor."

Gus nodded and glanced at the television. "Twenty bucks says he's not the father."

Pops grinned from the bed. "You're on."

In the end, Gus handed the money over to Pops, who chuckled as he put it in his wallet. "The baby has his eyes. Of course he's the father."

Gus shrugged, then took a seat at the end of Cec's bed, looking over at Pops. "Your color is looking pretty good, Burt. I'd say that nap this morning helped."

"That and the bear claw you brought me from the bakery." Pops smacked his lips. "That sure hit the spot."

"Glad I could help."

"You could help me even more if you took my granddaughter out for a little bit. It looks like she could use some air."

Gus glanced over his shoulder at Cec. "I can stay here with Burt if you want to get out of the room."

"You're not hearing him. He wants us both to go."

Gus turned back to Pops. "I don't think that staying here by yourself is such a good idea."

"Exactly what I said."

Pops looked at them both, his eyes narrowing. "And I said that I'm too old for a babysitter. Besides, what trouble could I possibly get into in this room?" He swept his arms around. "I'm really tired and would like some peace and quiet to get in a real nap. Between the both of you snoring last night, I didn't get much sleep."

"I do not snore." Cec rose from the pillows to glare at Pops. *He should talk. He's the one who sounded like he was cutting down trees with a chainsaw all night.*

"Actually, you do," said Gus, who turned toward her, a smile twitching around his lips. "I heard the evidence myself."

"Well, if I do, then the both of you do too. I'm not the only guilty one in this room."

"My point is that I could use a little time to myself. And I promise I'll stay in this room. And keep Hemingway here close to my side." He patted the tall oxygen cylinder that stood next to the bed.

Cec glanced at Gus, who gave her a shrug. "We wouldn't have to be gone long."

She knew she shouldn't agree, but she found herself nodding slowly. "Fine. But only for an hour. Tops."

Pops covered the side of his mouth and said to Gus, "I'll give you your twenty back if you make it two."

Gus shook his head. "I wouldn't push it."

Cec grabbed a gauzy short-sleeve blouse from her suitcase to wear over her tank top, then picked up her sandals from the floor at the side of the bed. Once dressed, she placed a kiss on Pops's whiskery cheek. "Stay out of trouble. I'll bring you back a sandwich or something for lunch."

"Pastrami if they have it."

"Extra mustard?"

Pops gave her a wink, then she turned to

find Gus watching them. He held out his arm to let her exit first.

Once outside, Cec turned to Gus. "What do you think that was about? He's up to something the way he keeps pushing the two of us together."

Gus chuckled and put his arm around her shoulder, steering her toward the stairway that would take them down to the parking lot. "You're overthinking this. It's just like he said. He's overtired and needs a bit of peace and quiet for a little while."

"Uh-huh." But she wasn't convinced.

They started walking across the parking lot toward the street. Gus pointed to the left. "I've already explored the street the other way. Let's see what's down here."

They walked in silence and waited at the corner for the light to turn so they could cross. When the light changed, Gus put a hand on her lower back as they entered the street. The gesture felt gentlemanly. Respectful. And Cec wondered if Tom had ever done anything like that when they were dating or later when they were married. She couldn't remember one, if he had. And the last couple years of their marriage,

Tom had been distant. Cold. Gus, on the other hand, was kind. Considerate.

Then she asked herself why that mattered. She wasn't interested in Gus. He was here today, gone tomorrow. He'd already admitted he wasn't the marrying kind any more, and he also planned on moving away soon. Zero out of ten. Would not recommend.

So then why did her fingers tingle every time her hand swung close to his? Why was she aware of his every movement as they walked side by side, their gazes straight ahead?

The businesses quickly turned to residential homes. Cec glanced around. "Maybe we should head back the other way? I don't think we'll find a place for lunch in this direction."

"I didn't realize that was where we were walking to."

"We'll pick up lunch and take it back to the room. We've been gone long enough."

Gus nodded, and at the next corner, they crossed the street and walked back the way they'd come. "You like to have goals to work toward, don't you?" he asked once they were on the other side.

"There's nothing wrong with that."

"And there's nothing wrong with taking a walk for the sake of enjoying a little exercise on a beautiful day."

"I didn't want to leave Pops alone, so I don't see the point of walking just for the sake of walking."

She didn't notice that Gus had stopped walking until she reached the next corner and realized she was alone. She turned back to find him watching her, his head cocked to one side as if he was trying to figure her out. She walked back to where he stood. "What?"

"You don't like me."

"I never said that."

"Or maybe it's that you do like me. Maybe more than you'd like to."

She rubbed her forehead with one hand. "My personal feelings for you have nothing to do with my wanting to get back to the motel room and Pops."

Gus grinned at her. "So, you admit that you do have feelings for me."

"Don't put words in my mouth."

He took a step toward her and stared at her, his eyes gazing at her lips. She bit her lip, then turned back and started walking toward the motel. Soon, he was beside her again. He slipped his hand in hers before they crossed the street and held on to it. She didn't understand why she continued to walk like this with him, but it felt comfortable. Natural.

She tried to tell herself the zing that went up her spine meant nothing.

After several discussions about where to order lunch, they settled on an ice cream stand called the Dairy Maid that also sold burgers and chili dogs. "Pops asked for pastrami, which they don't serve here."

"So, we will pick up a sandwich for him from the deli by the motel. Come on, Cecily. Live a little."

She narrowed her eyes at him but agreed. Once they received their order, they settled at a picnic table that overlooked a park and a slice of sandy beach beyond that. Gus handed her a burger and she unwrapped it and took a large bite. She closed her eyes and smiled, marveling at how good it tasted. When she opened her eyes to take another bite, she found Gus watching her with a smirk. "What?"

"I always pictured you as a salad person. Eat healthy. Live healthy. You know."

"There's nothing wrong with enjoying a burger every once in a while." She snagged a french fry from his side of the table. "Or a fry."

"I didn't say there was." He held the paper cup of fries toward her. "Please. Help yourself."

She took a few more and placed them on the paper wrapper next to her burger. "Thank you."

He gave her a nod. "I can be a nice guy sometimes."

"I didn't say…" She sighed and peered at him. "You're trying to get a rise out of me. To what? Distract me from my worries?"

"Is it working?"

"Can we be serious for a minute?" When he nodded and leaned in closer to her, she did too. "This morning scared me."

"I know."

"I mean, it really scared me. I thought he was dead. Or close to, at least." She put her burger down on the wrapper, her appetite lost somewhere in the dread from the morning's events. "Sometimes when we're home, I'll walk into the room and think, 'Is this the moment I discover he's gone?' As if I'm just waiting for him to…"

She let her words trail off, but he finished her thought for her. "To die. It's okay to say the word."

She shook her head. "No. Saying it makes it seem as if it's more likely to happen. At least, to me it does. I know what you said before."

He remained silent, but she felt his warmth, his concern. She looked down at her hands. "How much longer does he have?"

Gus didn't answer right away, so she looked up to find him staring out at the beach and the blue water of the Great Lakes beyond that. When he turned back to her, his eyes looked sad. And tired, but mostly sad. "I'm not a doctor."

"Just give me your best guess."

Gus shifted awkwardly, then swallowed. "Too soon."

She nodded. She'd known what he was going to say. And any length of time he'd said would still mean the same thing. Too soon.

"Cecily…" She stared into those sad eyes. He reached across the table for her hand. "I know you want to make his last days as comfortable and safe as possible. And I know you're scared that this trip will somehow make him worse. But that's the thing. He needs to go on this journey, and he's asked the two of us to come with him. That means something to me."

"To me too." She placed her hand in his.

"So why don't we make a pact that going forward we will help give him the best time possible. Whatever that means. And make sure he finishes his journey."

Cec wanted to argue. Wanted to say that the more important thing was to keep Pops safe. Protected. Alive.

But she knew Gus was right. Pops needed to travel this road for some reason. And he'd asked the two of them to go with him. To help him get to the end.

She squeezed his hand. "Okay. You've got a deal."

THE NIGHT PASSED without incident, and they were on the road by eight the following morning with bear claws and large to-go cups of coffee from the bakery near the motel. Burt had insisted he would sit in the back seat after their first rest stop a couple hours into the trip, so Cecily was beside Gus. He could smell the floral scent of her shampoo and conditioner wafting from her hair, which she wore up in a ponytail since the weather promised to be a scorcher. He glanced at her briefly, then looked in the rearview mirror to find Burt watching him, an amused expression on the older man's face.

Gus put his gaze back on the road. His talk with Cecily over lunch the day before seemed to have given her a calmness. Peace, maybe? She didn't follow Burt with anxious eyes or make comments that betrayed her inner anxiety. Maybe she had finally gotten to a sense of acceptance. He hoped she had. It would make what came later easier.

"According to my calculations, we should reach the motel we're staying at by five, and Lighthouse Bay is about a half-hour drive past that." She looked up from the notebook she'd been poring over. "That is, as long as we don't have side trips or incidents before then."

Gus couldn't help himself. "Now why do you have to go and jinx us like that?"

She gave a sniff. "I don't believe in jinxes."

"That doesn't mean they don't occur." He gripped the steering wheel tighter. "Growing up, my dad always said don't tempt fate."

"Well, Pops always said we make our own luck, fate, whatever."

"Yes, I did," Burt said from the back seat. "And if we do need to make a few stops on the way, there's nothing wrong with that."

Cecily turned in the seat to look at her grandfather. "I think we should be more concerned about getting to the motel for the night."

Gus reached over and put a hand over hers. She looked at where their hands were touching, her chin tilted up and she then gave him a small nod. "But if you want to stop somewhere, then by all means ask Gus, since he's driving."

"You're doing great," Gus whispered from the side of this mouth.

"I'm trying," she answered just as softly.

He squeezed her hand briefly then returned his to the steering wheel.

As they drove farther north, the hum of the tires on the road and the monotony of the trees and fields they passed put him into a slight stupor. He had to blink several times when his eyes got heavy. The snores from the back seat told him that Burt had fallen asleep. He glanced at his passenger beside him to find that she too had been taken captive by the warm air and tedium of the landscape. Her head had drooped to the side closest to Gus, inches away from his shoulder. If he didn't have a console between them, he would have pulled her closer to him.

He gave a big yawn and sat up straighter. *Got to stay awake.* He turned up the volume on the radio and changed the station to one that played a fast rock-and-roll beat. He tapped his fingers on the steering wheel and hummed along to the song. *Stay awake.*

Cecily stirred beside him, then gave a big yawn before opening her eyes as she stretched. She turned toward him and blinked a few more times. "Where are we?"

He lowered the volume on the radio. "The last big town we passed was Marquette, and that was about an hour ago." He pointed out the window on her side where she could catch glimpses of Lake Superior beyond the line of trees next to the two-lane highway. "We have about another hour to Houghton and then another hour after that."

She stretched and yawned again. "I didn't mean to fall asleep, but to keep you company while you drove."

"That's okay. If I didn't have to drive, I would be joining the both of you in slumberland." He pointed at the back seat. "Burt has been out most of the afternoon."

"Do you think we could stop soon to find a restroom?"

"Sounds good."

"And maybe I could take over driving for a while and give you a break."

"You don't have to do that."

She peered at him. "Worried that I'll somehow mess up your precious SUV? I'm a very good driver."

"I'm sure you are, but I'm good. I appreciate the offer."

They drove in silence for a while until a whining noise sounded beneath him. He turned off the radio. "Did you hear that?"

She looked at him as he strained to hear the noise again. Nothing. He was about to sigh when the whining noise sounded louder. And was followed by the steering wheel starting to shake. What in the world was going on?

"What's wrong with the car?"

He shook his head and tried to keep the steering wheel steady. Then a pop sounded, and steam emitted from the front of the car. He groaned and glanced behind them before easing the SUV onto the soft shoulder. He turned off the car and popped the button on the hood before getting out and walking toward the front of the car.

He found the latch to open the hood, then cursed as steam heated his fingers as he lifted it and looked inside. Cecily appeared beside him. "What happened?"

He shrugged. "I'm a medic, not a mechanic. But my best guess is that it's something with the engine. Since that's where all this steam is coming from."

Cecily took a long look under the hood

and shook her head. She grabbed her cell phone from the pocket of her shorts.

"Who are you calling?" he asked.

She looked up at him. "Triple A. I always pay for the service in case my car breaks down." She frowned and glanced at her phone. "I'm not getting a signal." She lifted her cell phone in the air and walked a little ahead. "Nothing."

Gus grabbed his phone, but the same thing happened. No signal. "We must be in a dead zone or something. I'm not getting anything either."

She groaned. "So, what do we do?"

Gus looked around at the road, but no cars appeared in either direction. "I guess we wait for someone to come along."

"For what? A miracle? This isn't exactly a busy highway where we can flag down a car. When's the last time you saw a car?"

"Maybe a half hour ago."

She closed her eyes and tilted her head back. "What else could possibly go wrong on this road trip?"

"I told you not to jinx it."

She narrowed her eyes at him and stalked back to the passenger door and got in. He could see her turn toward the back, probably letting Burt know what trouble they had gotten into now. He walked to the side of the car, and Burt rolled down the window beside him. "Engine trouble?"

"Seems to be."

Burt gave a shrug. "Ah well. What can you do?"

"We passed a town about five miles back or so. I could walk in that direction and see if I can find someone to help us."

Cecily seemed skeptical from the front seat. "And what if someone stops to help us while you're gone? I don't have a phone signal to let you know."

"What do you want to do? Wait and hope for the off chance that a Good Samaritan shows up to give us a hand?"

"It's better that we all stay together, and Pops can't be walking a long distance. So, we stay with the car."

"Baby girl, it could be hours."

"Then it takes hours." She peered at the both of them. "We stay together."

Burt looked at Gus, who gave a sigh and held up one finger. "I'll agree to wait an hour. But after that, I'm going for help."

Gus rolled down the windows to let a breeze in since the air conditioning was off, while Cecily retrieved an oxygen tank from the back to help Burt breathe. Without the radio on, silence fell on the group. Finally, Burt suggested trying to name all the states and their capitals to pass the time. Cecily, in turn, proposed playing the alphabet game, but neither idea took hold.

Ten minutes before Gus's hour deadline ended, a truck appeared in the distance coming in their direction from the other side of the road. Gus got out of the car and started to wave his arms, hoping to get the attention of the driver. The truck passed them. Well, shoot. He'd hoped the driver would take pity and stop.

He turned to find the truck making a U-turn, then it pulled up behind their SUV. A tall man who appeared to be in his mid-fifties popped out of the driver's side door and said, "Hey, folks. Having some trouble?"

Gus took a few steps toward him. "I think it's the engine."

"Mind if I take a look? I'm not a professional mechanic, but I know a fair amount from trying to fix my own trucks."

Gus waved the man forward to go ahead and look at the engine. He bent his head under the hood and made some *mmm-hmm*s and *uh-huh*s. There was even a *well now*. Finally, he let out a deep sigh and faced Gus. "It's the engine, all right. But I'm afraid it's beyond my limited skills to fix."

Great. "Do you know somewhere I can have it towed to get it fixed?"

The man paused, then gave a slow nod. "Sure. I can take you to a buddy of mine. He owns a garage a ways up the road here." He waved at Burt and Cecily still in the car. "With my wife along, there's not enough room in the truck for all y'all, but I could come back later for the rest of your group here."

Gus stuck out his hand. "Thank you...?"

"Steve. The wife's name is Amy." The man shook his hand. "And you?"

Gus pointed to himself. "Gus. And that's Burt and Cecily in the truck. We were heading to Lighthouse Bay."

"Oh, yes. Beautiful spot there."

"Burt grew up there, and he wanted to visit."

Steve peered into the truck again. "I tell you what. Why don't I drive you up to Mick's garage, and then I'll take the rest of your family to my place while you wait to get your car fixed?"

"I couldn't ask you to do that."

"You're not asking. I'm offering. Besides, Amy wouldn't let me back in the house if I didn't do the neighborly thing and offer her the chance to dote on y'all." Steve gave a nod. "I'll meet you at my truck when you're ready to go."

Gus watched the other man walk back to his truck. Cecily stuck her head out the window and beckoned him over. "Is he going to help us?"

"He's going to drive me to the garage up ahead. It's not far. Then he'll come back for you and Burt. He's invited you to stay at his house until I can make arrangements for a tow truck and get the engine fixed."

Cecily made a face. "If it's an engine issue, I don't think that's something even the best mechanic will be able to fix in a couple of hours." She checked her watch. "And it'll be dark before we know it and where are we going to stay the night? Did this guy happen to mention how close we are to the next motel?"

"Cecily." Gus put a hand on one of hers that was gripping the edge of the window. "One step at a time. I'll call you as soon as I can. Once we have all the information, then we can make some decisions."

Gus could see an artery on her forehead throb in tempo with her heartbeat. Finally, she sighed. "Fine."

"Good. I'll call you."

CEC SAT CLOSEST to the passenger door, Pops in the middle, with their new friends Amy and Steve driving the pickup. He pointed out the window. "If you peek through the trees, you can see the lake. It's beautiful on a day like today."

She didn't care about how the lake looked. She cared about getting to Lighthouse Bay. Or at least the motel they were supposed to be checking into for the next few days. She cared about Pops fulfilling whatever his mission was in coming to his hometown. Forget the lake.

But she made a noise of consent as Pops looked past her. "Check out those waves.

When I was a boy, I remember how calm the lake surface would be in the summer." He gave a chuckle. "That is until one of the freighters passed us and we'd be bobbing up and down like corks."

Steve chuckled. "Gus said you're from Lighthouse Bay."

"Born and raised. You from here?"

"Raised in Georgia, but I moved up here almost twenty years ago when my wife's folks got sick. They left us the farm, and we've been here ever since."

"What kind of farm do you have?" Cec asked.

Amy turned to look at her. "Corn mostly. But we've been branching into oats and barley too."

They nodded and fell into silence. Steve pulled into a dirt lane that led through the trees for a while before opening up into a meadow with a farmhouse and a bright blue barn. Fields of green beyond the buildings stretched as far as Cec could see. "This is a big farm."

Steve smiled. "It's been good to us."

He pulled the truck in front of the house and came around to help first Cec down, then Pops and his tank. Amy looked out towards a large garden that sat closer to the house. "Well, I'd better pick some more beans from the garden for dinner."

Dinner? Cec didn't plan on them staying that long. She'd wait for Gus's call, and then she'd make arrangements for them to stay at a motel. She shook her head. "That's not really necessary. We'll pick something up for dinner in town."

"Nonsense. You'll stay for dinner. I'll be right back." And Amy strode off toward the garden.

Cec looked to Steve who gave a shrug. "I'd recommend tasting Amy's cooking. You won't get a meal half as good anywhere else."

Pops glanced at Cec then to Steve, nodding. "We appreciate the offer. It's more than we expected."

"I bet you're thirsty after being stuck on the side of the road for so long. We have a pitcher of iced tea in the fridge. How about a glass?"

"Is it sweet tea?" Pops asked.

"Is there any other kind?"

Pops approached the first few steps that

led up to the porch. Cec stepped forward to take his arm and help him, but he waved her off. "I'm fine, baby girl."

Cec watched him climb the stairs and then took a deep breath. She noticed Steve watching her.

"It's all going to be okay, you know?" he said.

"Excuse me?"

"Your husband will get the car fixed, and you'll get back on your trip. But until then, why not just enjoy this little detour?"

"Gus isn't my husband. And did he tell you to say that? About the detour?"

"Oh. I assumed he was." Steve began walking. "Well, still. Why don't we go inside and get a glass of that sweet tea? You'll see, things will work out."

Cec gave a nod, then paused for another moment. This trip wasn't going at all to plan. Why should she be surprised that they'd had something else happen to keep them from their destination? She walked up the steps and into the house. Pops took a seat in a recliner as Steve brought him a glass of iced tea. He turned to Cec. "Can I get you a glass?"

Might as well settle in until they heard from Gus. "Yes, please." She asked Pops, "Are you feeling okay?"

"Never better."

Cec knew he would act like he felt better than he really did around others. He could reveal his true condition to her, her mother and Gus, which she was grateful for, but even to the doctors he would downplay his symptoms. That part made things more of a challenge. She took a seat on the sofa next to the recliner, which looked very similar to his at home.

Amy returned from the garden and joined them in the living room, sitting next to Cec on the sofa. Steve brought a tall glass of iced tea for her and handed another to Amy. His wife patted his hand. "Thanks, love."

Steve leaned down and kissed her cheek. "I'd better check that hose out back before dinner."

He nodded to the others, walked through the house and out the back. In a moment, the pickup truck roared to life.

Amy turned to Cec. "So where are you folks headed to?"

"My hometown of Lighthouse Bay," Pops answered. "Ever heard of it?"

"Steve took me to the lighthouse a few years ago for my birthday. Small town, but lovely. You grew up there?"

Pops shared stories of his boyhood as Cec checked and rechecked her cell phone. *Come on, Gus.* He should have some kind of news by now, shouldn't he? Why hadn't he called yet? Hearing nothing made her more nervous than if he had called with bad news. The longer she waited, the more she fretted. What if the mechanic couldn't fix the engine? What were they going to do then? Where would they stay? And for how long?

Cec turned to Amy when she realized the woman had asked her a question. "I'm sorry. I didn't catch that."

"Burt was telling me you followed his footsteps into teaching. I asked what grade you taught."

"High school math, mostly algebra and precalculus."

Amy gave a whistle. "Impressive. I barely squeaked by in math, but English? Ahh, that's where I excelled."

Pops lit up. "That was my best subject. Who is your favorite author?"

They started discussing books, and it turned out that Amy had once been a librarian back in Georgia before moving north. With Pops and Amy talking about all things books, Cec knew she could concentrate on her plan for what came next.

Her phone started to buzz, and she stood and pointed to the front door. "I'll just step outside and take this."

She answered as she exited onto the porch. "Gus? Tell me you have good news." Silence. She closed her eyes. She knew it wouldn't be good. "Gus? Are you there?"

"It's going to be a few days before Mick can fix it. And since we're heading into a holiday weekend, it's likely going to be a week."

"A week?" Her cry stopped the conversation in the living room, and she walked farther away from the front door. "Gus, what are we supposed to do for a week while we wait for it to be fixed?"

"There's a car rental place a few towns over. They're closed for the day now, but we could call in the morning and rent a car.

Drive to Lighthouse Bay. And we can return it on our way back when we pick up my car."

"Gus…"

"It's not perfect, but it's the best idea I have right now. Because you're right. We can't wait around here for a week. We don't have that kind of time."

At least they agreed on that. "I'll tell Pops. And I'll start calling motels in the area to see if anyone has a couple of rooms."

"Ah… Mick says there isn't a motel around here. There are some cabins we could have rented, but they're already booked for the summer season."

Great. "I'll figure something out." She turned to find that Amy had joined her on the front porch. "I better let you go."

"Mick said he'd drop me off at Steve's place. We'll make our plans together, okay?"

She hung up the phone after telling him goodbye. She looked over at Amy. "The engine can't be fixed for a while, so we'll have to rent a car to get to Lighthouse Bay."

"You're planning on driving there tonight? You'll never get a rental car at this time of day." Amy pointed inside. "I tell you what. We have the kids' bedrooms that are empty. You'll stay tonight with us, and Steve will get you to the car rental place tomorrow morning."

"We couldn't impose on you."

"Nonsense. It's been too quiet around here since our youngest got married and moved out. I'd enjoy the company, however temporary." Amy smiled warmly at Cec and Cec realized her defenses were weakening. "You can get a good night's rest here, and things won't look so bleak in the morning."

"I really don't think..." But what other options did they have?

"I'm not taking no for an answer." Amy stared at her until Cec gave a short nod. "Good. Do you play cards? After dinner, we could get a couple of games going. I haven't had a chance to beat anyone at cards in a very long time."

Amy steered Cec inside the house, and she had a feeling that anything she might have said would have been overruled anyway.

AFTER DINNER AND several hands of cards where Amy beat them all, Gus shook his head and pushed back his chair. He glanced at Burt, who seemed to be enjoying losing.

Amy glanced at them all as she shuffled the cards. "How about we switch to Michigan Rummy?"

Cecily held up a hand. "I think I need a little break. I want to go look at the stars outside since it's such a clear night. We don't get a view like this down in the suburbs."

"Oh, sure. A starry sky is one of the best things about living out here." Amy began putting the cards away.

Everyone stood. Steve stretched his arms over his head. "That's enough for me tonight."

Cecily left the room, and a moment later they could hear the front screen door open then close. Burt turned to Gus and nodded his head toward where Cecily had gone. Gus got the message, but didn't really need the encouragement. Being alone with Cecily was often on his mind these days.

Gus found Cecily sitting on the front steps, staring up at the pretty night sky. The light from the waxing moon shone down and lit up the planes of her face.

"Look, it's Orion's Belt."

Gus glanced upward as he took a seat

next to her. "I thought you were into math, not astronomy."

"Can't I be interested in both? I'm a multifaceted woman." She pointed to another collection of stars that formed a W. "Cassiopeia."

"Are you trying to impress me with your knowledge of constellations?"

She glanced at him, then nudged him with her shoulder. "More like trying to make up for my clear lack of skills playing cards."

"More like we were playing with a pro than any comment on our ability."

"Maybe." She chuckled, then took a deep breath and sighed as she let out the air. "I think this is the first moment I haven't felt worried about Pops since we started this trip."

"Really? Even with the car troubles? And throwing your schedule out the window and having everything up in the air?" Gus nudged her shoulder. "I'm finding that a little hard to believe."

"This clean air is probably doing more for him than anything I could have done at home. Sounds corny, huh? Besides, I didn't say I wasn't worried about how we're going to get to Lighthouse Bay and whatever else lies ahead of us on this adventure."

"You're seeing it as an adventure now."

"Trying to." She glanced up at the sky again before turning to look at him. "Someone told me I need to enjoy the journey more."

He looked into her eyes. "Sounds like a really wise man."

"Meh."

She smiled wide and he felt his chest tighten. He reached up and pushed back a strand of hair that had fallen out of her ponytail, then let his thumb linger on her cheek. He started to lean in to kiss her, but the front door squeaked as Steve stepped onto the porch. "Don't mean to interrupt, but Burt is ready to get to bed."

Cecily started to stand, but Gus beat her to it. "I'll take care of him. You enjoy the stars for a little longer."

She smiled at him again, then brought her knees up a step and put her arms around her legs. He watched her for a moment longer before leaving to take care of Burt.

CHAPTER EIGHT

CEC WAVED OFF the offer of another spoonful of scrambled eggs. "I'm stuffed but thank you. These are the lightest I've ever had. What's your secret?"

"Don't overcook the eggs. And having the freshest eggs doesn't hurt either," Amy answered as she slid two more pieces of bacon onto Gus's plate. He thanked her and added more butter and maple syrup to his already tall stack of pancakes alongside his eggs.

"I appreciate the praise almost as much as how empty your plates will be."

Cec glanced at the plates that still had enormous amounts of food on them and looked over at Amy, who winked at her from the stove. "Trust me. It will happen."

"I don't know how we'll ever be able to repay your kindness for letting us stay and feeding us like this." Cec tried to calculate what it would have cost them if they hadn't spent the night there.

"We didn't help you in order to get paid back."

"Still, I feel like we should give you something for all you've done for us."

Amy took a seat at the table with her own full breakfast plate. "And I feel like I should give you folks something for joining us. It gets lonesome with the kids out on their own now. Sure, they'll visit, but it's not the same as having them under our roof." She paused and looked at the group. "So maybe I should be the one paying you."

"Well, thank you. It meant a lot for us to find a place to stay."

After breakfast, Gus helped Amy wash dishes as Cec got ready for them to leave. She double-checked the bedrooms they had stayed in to make sure that everything they had brought had been packed. When she returned to the main floor, she found Pops dozing on the overstuffed sofa in the living room. She walked over to him and placed a hand on his. He blinked several times, then looked at her. "Is it time to leave?"

"Almost. Are you feeling okay?"

He nodded, then closed his eyes. "I don't think I've ever slept so well as I did last night. Must be all the fresh air blowing through the open windows."

"Must be."

"Even made my dreams sweeter." He opened his eyes. "I dreamed of your grandmother last night. She was standing on the opposite shore of a lake, waving at me. She looked exactly like she did when I first met her all those years ago. I think she's waiting for me to join her. And I have a feeling it's going to be soon."

"Pops…"

"I know, I know. You don't like talking about it." He gave a grunt as he started to stand up. "I'd best visit the gentleman's before we head out."

Cec brought his walker closer so he could manage down the hall. She watched his slow progress, then took a deep breath and wiped the tear away from the corner of her eye.

"Cecily, we should be leaving soon."

She turned to find Gus standing next to her. She gave a nod then. "I already checked that we packed everything."

He looked concerned. "Are you okay?"

No. But Pops needed her to be. "I will be once we get on the road again. We can probably make Lighthouse Bay by lunchtime."

"Ahh, there's my official planner. I was wondering where she had gone to. But I think I'll miss my stargazer."

She remembered how they had almost kissed the night before. She also remembered how she would have welcomed it. Had wanted it. She licked her bottom lip, then dismissed the image in her head. "She's still here, but the official planner would like to make sure we accomplish what we set out to do on this trip."

"All in due time."

BURT APPLAUDED AT the sight of the sign announcing Lighthouse Bay town limits. "Go up here a little ways, then turn left at the blinking red light and that will take us right into the heart of the town."

But the blinking red light had been replaced by a traffic light in the years that Burt had been gone. He marveled at it as Gus turned the SUV onto the street that was tree-lined with houses for about a half mile before the trees thinned out and the business district appeared. Gus spotted one very important place. "There's Graham's General Store, Burt. Ready to see if Phyllis is there?"

Burt peered out the window and shook his head. "I'm starting to get cold feet now that we're here. What if she hasn't forgiven me, after all these years, for breaking up with her to join the navy? What if she tells me off? And to be fair, she'd have every right to."

Cecily leaned over the back seat and put a hand on Burt's shoulder. "We don't have to rush into anything."

"Or maybe it's better to rip off that bandage quick." Gus parked and opened his door. "Whatever you decide, Burt, I need to stretch my legs. I'm going to take a walk."

Gus hadn't gone far before Burt called, "Wait!" Gus turned back to look at him. Burt stared out the SUV window at the façade of the building and gave a nod. "Best to do it quick."

Gus helped Burt out of the car and hooked up the portable oxygen machine to the walker. "Be brave, Burt. You've got the right idea."

Burt nodded but his eyes stayed on the front door of the general store. He took one step then another. Gus and Cecily followed behind him. Cecily asked, "Are you sure this is a good idea? Maybe we should get some lunch first."

Gus moved past Burt to open the door for him, then held it open for Cecily as well. The general store was a large room with several packed aisles down the middle. Near the front, a cash register and counter stood in front of a large wall of shelves full of items meant for fishing and hunting. A young girl glanced up at them from her cell phone as they entered. "Welcome to Graham's."

Burt gasped. "Philly?"

The girl looked back at him, frowning. "Excuse me?"

Burt's expression was full of regret. "You look exactly like someone I knew a long time ago."

The girl nodded. "You're here for my grandmother, right? Everyone says I look just like her when she was my age."

"If Phyllis is your grandmother, then they are right."

Cecily stepped forward. "Is your grandmother here today?"

"No, it's her day off."

Burt's face fell, and he leaned against his walker. "That's what I was afraid of. I should have contacted her. Should have let her know I was coming."

"But I can give her a call and ask her to come by. Who should I say is asking after her?"

Burt walked closer to the counter and gave the girl his name. She dialed her grandmother's number and waited for her to answer. As the two chatted, Gus took a stroll down an aisle. It held household cleaners next to gardening supplies next to rain ponchos. He turned the corner to walk up the next aisle to find Cecily approaching him. "Phyllis has asked that we bring Pops to her house for lunch. Are you in?"

It could be interesting to meet the woman who had made Burt travel hundreds of miles to see her one last time. Phyllis had been a lot of what they'd been talking about these last couple of weeks. She had to be something if Burt still had feelings for her all these years later. "Definitely."

CEC WASN'T SURE what she expected Phyllis to be like, but it wasn't the tall, thin woman with white hair who blinked at her from behind her large spectacles. Maybe because her grandmother had been so petite, barely five foot. Or because Phyllis even now towered over her grandfather. But the look in his eyes as he watched her move around her kitchen proved that she was Phyllis. "Lunch was lovely," she said.

Phyllis waved her hand at this compliment. "If I'd known you were coming, I would have made a more elaborate spread than this."

More elaborate than three different kinds of salads, rolls and a veggie tray with a creamy dip in the center? And if Cec's nose was correct, she'd baked something with chocolate for dessert. "You didn't need to go to all this trouble."

"Nonsense. It's the least I could do for an old friend." The older woman turned to look at Burt, staring at him for a long time, then shook her head. "Burt Karsten in my house after all these years. I would never have believed it."

Pops smiled and reached over to take her hand, pressing a kiss to it briefly. "You look just as beautiful."

"And you must have forgotten your glasses. I'm old."

"As am I."

Over lunch, Burt and Phyllis reminisced about different classmates of theirs, giving updates on them if they had information. Burt sighed as he recalled a particularly good friend of his who had died recently. "Seems like there's less and less of us around every year."

"It's the way life is, isn't it? The important thing is to hold on to those who are dear to you."

"I shouldn't have left you all those years ago."

"You had to leave just as much as I had to stay." Phyllis glanced at Cec. "Besides, if you hadn't left Lighthouse Bay, this beautiful young woman wouldn't be sitting at this table." She reached over and patted Burt's hand. "I hope you had a good life."

"I did. A good job, a good marriage and family. You?"

"Les was a good man, and we had four lovely children. Three sons and a daughter. I have thirteen grandchildren, and I was just made a great-grandmother for the third time this past Christmas."

"Grandchildren are a blessing, that's for sure." He turned to wink at Cec.

Gus shifted in his chair. "I've really enjoyed lunch, Phyllis. But while you visit with Burt, would you excuse Cecily and me? We need to find a motel, then get checked in for the night."

Burt frowned. "What happened to our reservation?"

Cec shrugged. "They canceled it after I tried to reschedule it again when we got stuck last night. I just hope we can find a place that has space open with the holiday weekend upon us."

Phyllis looked at them in surprise. "A motel? No, no, there's no need for that. We have a family cabin not far from here that no one is using right now. You'll stay there."

Cec replied first. "We couldn't take advantage of your hospitality like that."

"You can, and you will. It would be my pleasure to offer it to you." She stood and left the room, returning moments later with a set of keys. "I can draw you a map to the place so you can go get settled. But I think you're right. I'd like to talk to Burt some more. You don't mind if I steal him for a few hours?"

Burt nodded vigorously, and Cec smiled. "That sounds great."

Phyllis drew them a map, then Cec stood and gave Burt a kiss on his cheek. "I'll bring in an extra oxygen tank just in case. And we'll see you later?"

Once they were back on the road, Gus whistled. "Wow, Burt is still besotted with Phyllis."

Cec laughed at his use of the old-fashioned word. "Besotted? Maybe a little starry-eyed, but it's been almost seventy years since they've seen each other. It's a little soon for besotted."

"Is *gobsmacked* a better word? Because the man couldn't keep his eyes off the woman. And I say, good for Burt. It's nice to have a little something at his age."

"It's nice to have something at any age."

Gus glanced at the map, then pointed at the bright pink mailbox. "When she said to turn left at the pink mailbox, I wasn't sure I'd be able to find it but that's got to be it."

They drove a little farther along a narrow dirt road until the trees thinned out and opened onto a log cabin. "This is definitely not what I pictured when we made plans for this road trip," Cec said as she peered out the windshield at the charming wooden building. "A motel in the sticks, sure. But this? It looks like we'll discover Snow White inside."

"I think the dwarves had a cottage, not a cabin. But it is delightful." He turned to look at her. "Should we take a look inside?"

Inside the cabin, they found a large room styled in an open concept with the living area juxtaposed to the kitchen and dining room. Comfy couches and armchairs next to a long wooden table with mismatched chairs. Bookcases flanking a wood-burning stove. Steps to the left side of the living area led up to a loft that ran along the back wall of the cabin and boasted two small bedrooms with large king-size beds squeezed into the spaces. Cec fell in love with the room that had a window overlooking the back of the cabin, where a firepit was surrounded by chairs. She could see a glimpse of the lake farther beyond. "I'll take this room."

She could feel Gus standing behind her as he looked over her shoulder into the bedroom. "This is better than I expected."

"Agreed." She turned, and he stood right in front of her. He looked at her for a long moment, then took a step back and cleared his throat. "I should bring our luggage in from the car."

"I can help."

"I've got it." Then he fled down the stairs and out the door. She took a peek at the other bedroom, which also looked out over the firepit area. She wondered if they'd get a chance to sit there one evening. But then realized the danger of an open flame next to Pops's oxygen tank. Just beyond the firepit, she could see a hammock strung between two trees, swaying slightly in the breeze.

She returned downstairs to find that Gus had stacked their luggage close to the stairs. She retrieved her suitcase and took it upstairs with her. She placed it on a small table in the bedroom. There were no drawers or closet, so she left her clothes inside. Retrieving her cosmetic bag and toiletries from the suitcase, she realized they hadn't found a bathroom during their brief tour. Oh no! Were they meant to really rough it at the cabin?

Gus appeared in the doorway. "I emptied the car except for the extra oxygen tanks." He frowned at the look on her face. "What's wrong?"

"Where's the bathroom? Did you see it when we were looking around?"

"They've got to have one, right?"

They left the bedroom, but there was no bathroom on the top floor. Downstairs, they opened doors, searching. Cec paused. "You don't think they're so rustic that they have an outhouse, do you?"

Gus shook his head and pressed his hand on a panel on the wall. "No, I think they just hid the door for it." He pushed the panel back to reveal a small bathroom.

Cec leaned in next to him and examined the room. "This has to be the tiniest bathroom in the whole world."

"Space is at a premium here."

Cec turned to look at him and realized she was tight against him. She backed away and pushed a stray hair behind her ear. "It is a tiny cabin."

He glanced away, then took a deep breath. "So, we have the afternoon free, just the two of us. What would you like to do?"

"There's a lake not far from here. We could go swimming."

"Sounds nice, but unfortunately, I didn't pack swim trunks."

She gave him a sly smile. "I don't know about you, but the idea of taking a nap in that hammock out back has my vote."

Gus smiled back at her. "I'll race you for it."

She immediately pushed past him to get to the door that led to the back deck. She had reached the bottom step when two strong hands lifted her in the air and moved her aside so Gus could run ahead. He beat her to the hammock without breaking a sweat. Cec put her hands on her hips and bent forward to try to catch a breath. "You cheated."

Gus pointed at the hammock. "It looks

big enough for the both of us. What do you say?"

Very tempting. She visually measured the surface area, then tugged at the ropes that tied the hammock to the trees. "Seems like it could hold both of us. Let's give it a try."

They grinned as they each tried to sit on the edge of the hammock.

And flipped over to land on the dirt instead.

Gus stood and brushed off the back of his shorts then held out a hand to help her to her feet. "That did not go as planned."

"I think we need to evenly distribute our weight. Each one of us get on one side and time it so that we balance each other."

"Right."

She walked to the other side and glanced behind her to find Gus watching her. He winked at her before he turned his back, so she did the same. "Okay. One. Two. Three."

On three, they each sat on the hammock. It swung but stayed upright as they cautiously moved farther onto it. Cec raised her legs up and lay back to stare at the sky. Gus's legs landed beside her arms. She lifted her head to find him lying on the other end, arms stretched over his head and eyes closed. It made for better weight distribution to lie that way, but she couldn't squelch the disappointment of not being able to lay her head against his shoulder.

She closed her eyes and took a deep breath of air that smelled like pine and lake and sunshine. Any thoughts in her head soon drifted away, and she sighed and let her body relax.

A SHADOW FELL over Gus's face, and he blinked for a few moments until he realized that Pops loomed beside him. "That looks mighty comfortable."

"You should try it."

"I'd end up in the dirt."

"Oh, we did that the first time. You should have seen it." He started to move, but realized his movements made the hammock sway. He brought his head up to see that Cec still slept. "What time is it?"

"Almost five. I came to let you know that Phyllis is taking me out to dinner, so the two of you are on your own. Is that okay?"

Gus grinned and squeezed Burt's hand.

"That's why we came all this way, isn't it?" He peered at the older man. "So how is it going so far between the two of you?"

Burt shrugged, but a blush started to bloom on his cheeks. "Pretty good, I guess. She wants to talk more over dinner, so that's got to be something, right?"

"I'd say so."

"And she doesn't seem to mind the oxygen tank as a chaperone." Burt glanced at Cecily and then at Gus. "What about you and my sweet granddaughter? How is that going?"

"Burt..."

"I'm not blind, so I know how you look at her." He paused. "And how she looks at you too."

Cecily looked at him? Gus cleared his throat. "There's nothing going on. Yet."

"Well, you take her out tonight for dinner. To a really nice place. And then see where the night takes you."

"Is that your plan with Phyllis?"

Burt winked at him. "Speaking of her, I'd better get back up to the cabin. I told her I would only be a moment."

"Are you sure you can walk that far?"

"I made it here just fine." He patted the tank next to him. "Hemingway gave me a hand on the grass. My walker would never have gotten out here."

"Still. Maybe I should help you get back."

"Don't you dare. You'll disturb Sleeping Beauty over there." He patted Gus's shoulder, then started the slow trek back to the deck and up the three steps. He turned back and shouted, "Don't wait up for me."

Gus waved back at him, smiling. Cecily stirred on the other end of the hammock. "Was that Pops?"

"He's having dinner with Phyllis tonight, so you and I are on our own."

Cecily stretched and groaned. "That was the best nap I've had in a long time. How long were we asleep?"

"Over two hours." He peered at the hammock that swayed with their movements. "Have you thought about how we're going to get out of this without ending up face down on the ground?"

"Oh." She glanced around them, then tugged on the ropes on one side of the hammock. It started to tip, and she let the rope go. "I see your point. Guess we'll have to keep the weight distribution balanced and time our dismount."

"Well, if the worst happens, we know there's a shower to get cleaned up in before we go out tonight."

She looked at him. "We're going out?"

He nodded and gave her what he hoped was his best smile. "Let's explore this town a little. Didn't you have a list of places to eat around here?"

By the time they extricated themselves from the hammock, they had to shower and change before leaving for dinner.

CHAPTER NINE

CEC DRANK THE yeasty beer, then set the stein down on the wooden table that had a live edge. She ran her hand across the wood while she glanced around the restaurant and then across the table to her dinner date. Gus sat looking at her, and she reached up to push away a hair from her eyes. "The beer is good. I hope the food is just as tasty."

"Me too. I'm starving. No offense to Phyllis, but I need more than salads to get me through the day."

"We had rolls. And dessert."

"Actually, we left before she brought out dessert."

She gave him a shrug. "I'm sorry you got stuck with me for dinner."

"I'm not."

"And if today is any indication, you'll probably get stuck with me some more while Pops goes off with Phyllis."

"You don't hear me complaining, do you?" He leaned in a little closer to her. "But are you disappointed?"

"A little." At Gus's wince, she waved her hands. "No, not about you. But about not being able to spend time with Pops and see his hometown through his eyes."

"I don't think he plans on completely abandoning us."

"I hope not."

"But let's not worry about that. Tonight, let's just focus on good beer. Good food." He lifted his stein. "And good company, of course."

She lifted her stein and clinked it against his before taking another drink. "I'm not much of a beer drinker, but I'm enjoying this."

"Well, I drink a lot of beer, and this is very good."

"Gus Sheridan?" a voice called from another table. Cec turned toward the direction of the voice and saw a man likely in his mid-thirties approaching their table. "I thought that was you."

Gus stood and shook the guy's hand before bringing him closer to pat his back.

"Alex, what in the world are you doing in this neck of the woods?"

"I was about to ask you the same thing." Alex turned to look at Cec, then held out his hand. "Pardon me. I'm an old army buddy of Gus's. And you are?"

"Gus's neighbor, Cecily."

"Pleasure to meet you." He turned back to Gus. "So, what are you doing in the UP, man? Last I heard you were out in Arizona or Utah."

"I've been in Michigan the last few years, down near Detroit. You?"

"I own a resort up here. Hey, the two of you should stop by and check it out. It's about twenty minutes from here. I'd love to give you a tour."

"You own a resort?"

Alex shrugged off his words. "It's more like an overgrown lodge right on the lake, but resort makes it sound fancier. And fancy helps pay the bills."

"What happened to your plans to open a restaurant in New York?"

"My wife's father left the lodge to her when he died, so our plans changed."

"Wait. You got married?"

Alex laughed, then turned to signal to a woman to join them. Cec nodded at her as Gus kept shaking his head. "Gus, this is Rose. Rose, this is that guy I was telling you about the other day."

Rose grinned. "That's amazing, it must be fate to see you here then." She turned to Cec. "You must join our table. Unless…" She looked between them. "Are we interrupting a date?"

Gus hesitated. "No, not a date." He said to Cec, "You don't mind joining them, do you?"

She had been wondering what it was that was going on between her and Gus, but his words laid to rest any doubts. *Not a date.* Disappointing. But still, she smiled. "We'd love to join you."

Over dinner, Gus and Alex regaled the women with tales from the army and the high jinks they had gotten themselves in. Cec found herself laughing along with them and enjoying the meal as much as the company. After a couple of hours, she gave a yawn, though she tried to stifle it. Gus gave her a nod. "I should be getting us back to the cabin."

They stood, and the men shook hands while the women gave each other a quick hug. "It was a pleasure meeting you both," Cec said.

"How long are you in town for? You should really check out the resort," Rose told them. "I know Alex would love for you to see what he's done to the place, Gus. He's talked about getting a hold of you, and here you are."

Gus looked at Alex. "I'd love to see it." He turned to her. "Cec, do you think we could squeeze in a visit in the next few days?"

"I don't see why not."

Alex and Gus exchanged phone numbers with each other, then Gus ushered Cec out into the night air, which had gotten cooler since they'd arrived. Cec crossed her arms over her chest, splaying her hands over her bare arms. Gus put an arm around her and pulled her close to his side. "I'll keep you warm until we get to the rental car, okay?"

She murmured her consent, and they walked to where he had parked the rental SUV. He opened her car door first and waited for her to get inside before running around and sliding into the driver's seat.

Alex and Rose drove by and Gus gave a honk. "Man, I never thought I'd see Alex again. Thanks for being a sport and joining them tonight."

A sport. Yep, that was her. "They seem like a really nice couple."

"I'm having a hard time imagining him married, to be honest. I mean, this was the guy who would have a date with one woman in the afternoon then come home, shower and go out with another one that night. But I guess when you finally get bit by the love bug, you change your ways."

Cec glanced at him. "Have you ever changed for a woman?"

He considered her words as he put the car into gear and pulled out of the parking lot. "In my first marriage, I think I was too naïve about what it took to make a marriage work. By the time I got married the second time, I was too stubborn and set in my ways. But would I change in the future?" He knew what his heart was telling him. "For the right one, I think I would, yes. Would you?"

"I did. For Tom. And we both saw how that turned out."

He fixed his gaze back on the road. "How did you change for your ex?"

"I wanted children right away, but he talked me into waiting at least five years. I wanted to buy a house that we could choose together, but I moved into the one he already owned. I had planned on pursuing my PhD and teaching at the university level, but Tom persuaded me that I had enough education and a career path as a high school teacher was more stable and better for our relationship and for our someday family." She turned to look at him. "Should I continue?"

"No. You've made your point."

"And what was my point?"

"That you gave up your dreams for someone who didn't deserve you."

"No, that's not it. I changed my dreams for him."

"So, change them back to before your ex. Go and get that PhD. Buy your own house. As for the kids part, that's a little more complicated."

"I'm not the same person I was when I had those goals. To be honest, I don't know what I want anymore." She gazed out into the night. "Do you know?"

"I know what I don't want. But figuring out what I do is more intricate than stating I want to pursue a degree or buy a house. That's what the last few months have been about. Exploring what it is that makes me come alive."

"I'm guessing it's not medicine anymore."

"Correct. But what else do I have? If I don't use my medical background, does that mean I wasted all those years? And can I find satisfaction in medicine again, or am I completely burned out for good?" He signaled to change lanes and sped up. "You know what, I'd rather not talk about that right now. I'd like to focus on enjoying the rest of the evening and not get too deep."

"But isn't that your problem? You keep things light, and on the surface, but the answers are found deeper than you're willing to go."

"I didn't say I wasn't willing. I said I don't want to do it tonight."

"If not now, then when?"

"Cecily..."

"Why don't you ever call me Cec like Pops and all my friends do?" It seemed that he went out of his way to use her full name, and she'd been curious as to why.

He paused at a stop sign. "I didn't know you wanted me to." He glanced at her, then continued their drive. "Are we becoming friends?"

"I think we passed that threshold a while ago, don't you? At least at the beginning of this road trip. And if we are friends, then let me give you something to think about when you're trying not to think about it. Pops is proof that our time is limited, and if you're not doing what you love or enjoy, then what's the point?"

Gus didn't say anything to that and kept silent as they continued to the cabin.

Pops had returned by the time they arrived. He sat on the sofa, looking happy, but tired. "I figured I'll take the sofa down here since I don't think I can do those stairs."

"That's what we figured, so Gus left your suitcase down here where it would be easy to find." Cec sat on the sofa next to him. "So how did it go with Phyllis?"

"Wonderful. We made plans to spend tomorrow together. I hope you don't mind if I'm with her for the day instead of with you two."

"I thought we were going to look for your old house."

"We can do it another day, okay? I'd really like to see Phyllis again."

Cec nodded. "Sounds like she forgave you for leaving her."

Pops yawned instead of answering her. "I'll turn in now since tomorrow promises to be another big day. Would you check my air condenser to make sure it's plugged in before you go up to bed?"

After confirming everything was set for Pops, Cec used the bathroom to wash her face and put on her pajamas. She returned to the bedroom upstairs and sat on the edge of the bed. There was a soft knock on the door that could only be Gus. "Come in."

Gus stuck his head inside. "Since Burt is going to be with Phyllis for the day, would you mind if we check out Alex's resort tomorrow? I have to admit I'm curious about it after seeing him tonight."

"Sounds like a good idea. I don't think

Pops is interested in that, so it would be great timing."

"So, what do you think about him and Phyllis spending all this time together?"

Cec was confused. "It's nice, I guess. It's a shame that there's no future in it. You said so yourself that his time left is limited. I wish he had more."

"You have to admit that his color looks better tonight than it has in a long time. Phyllis could be good for him."

"No denying that."

"Well, good night. Sleep tight." He pushed off the door and gave a little wave.

"You, too."

She considered the new scenario as she lay on the bed and stared at the ceiling. Would Pops want to spend the rest of his days up here where he could be near Phyllis? Could Cec let him go or would she follow him here until the end? And why did the possibility of it make her a little more anxious than she already was?

GUS DIPPED THE oar into the water, focusing on Cecily as she did the same at the front of the canoe. Alex had given them both a tour of the resort, but it was just as he said. More like an overgrown lodge. The main room had taken up a lot of space with two staircases leading up on both sides behind the large reception desk. A huge dining room was located beyond the main room, and Alex had told them they served meals all day until midnight. Upstairs, there had to be at least fifty rooms for visitors to rent for the night. They offered outdoor activities such as swimming, fishing and canoeing. Bikes could be rented and ridden on the hiking trails around the resort. It was an outdoorsy person's dream vacation.

Alex had encouraged them to take a canoe out on the lake and get a feel for the property, then handed them a cooler with a packed lunch that now sat on the floor of the canoe between Gus's legs. "You about ready to stop somewhere for lunch?" he called to Cecily.

She nodded and pointed to the right where a small beach surrounded by trees waited. "We could take the canoe on shore over there."

They aimed the canoe in that direction and rowed it ashore. Gus stepped into the water and carried the canoe the rest of the way onto the beach, then pulled out the cooler and set it on the sand. "Let's see what they packed for us."

Inside were sandwiches, bags of chips, fresh veggies, homemade peanut butter cookies and bottles of water. Cecily picked out one of the bottles, twisted off the top and took several swigs. She took a deep breath and closed her eyes, lifting her head toward the sun above. "That was a workout."

"When's the last time you took a canoe out on the water?"

She opened her eyes to look at him. "The summer before my senior year of college. A group of us rented a cabin near Lake Michigan for a week. We also went tubing and swimming. It was an amazing time."

"You did pretty well for supposedly being rusty."

"So did you. When was the last time you did this?"

"Last summer. I backpacked through Northern Michigan for a couple weeks and rented a canoe to travel by water at one point."

"You're a real outdoors kind of person, aren't you?"

"I enjoy it. Just like I enjoy riding motorcycles through the Mojave Desert. Or hiking through Yellowstone Park. Or going fishing in the Mississippi River."

"You really have been everywhere."

"I don't see why I should tie myself down to just one place when there's so much of the world to see. Don't you ever want to leave Thora?"

"Sometimes but I've got family there. I like being near them"

"Well, I like travelling. Seeing new places, meeting new people. Sure, I've got family in Washington and Missouri, but that doesn't mean I have to live there."

"You don't talk much about your family."

He shrugged. "My parents split up when I was younger. My older sister Ruthie keeps in touch, and I visit when I can."

"Are you two close?"

"Not like we used to be. Sometimes…" He thought about Ruth and sighed. "Sometimes I wish we could be closer, but my parents' divorce had us choosing sides, and we ended up being on opposite teams."

"You're closer to your mom."

He nodded. "And my sister sided with my dad. We never really recovered from that."

Wanting to change the subject, he grabbed a sandwich and tossed it to her. "Let's eat, then explore the woods around here before we head back."

POPS REJECTED THEIR suggestion of sitting on the deck and stargazing when he returned home. "I'm having the time of my life, but it's wearing me out like you wouldn't believe. By the way, Phyllis and her family have a huge Fourth of July picnic each year at the beach, and we've been invited to join them. What do you think?"

Gus glanced at Cec, and she gave a nod. "I think that would be a great idea."

Pops smiled then squelched a yawn. He reached over and hugged her. "Good night, baby girl."

She put her arms around him and gave him a quick kiss on the cheek. "Get some rest. We'll be in to check on you in a little bit."

Since Pops wouldn't be joining them,

Gus suggested they build a fire in the pit. She agreed, so she searched the cabin's kitchen to find some marshmallows they could roast along with chocolate and graham crackers to make s'mores. She did find plenty of marshmallows and graham crackers, but she couldn't find chocolate bars, locating chocolate peanut butter cups instead. It would have to do.

She brought the supplies out on the deck, and Gus had built a wood tower that flames had just started to consume. He smiled as she placed the food on the small table between two of the wooden Adirondack chairs that flanked the fire pit. "We'll have to wait a little while for roasting marshmallows, but the anticipation will make it worth it."

Cec settled onto a chair and tipped her head back to take in the starry sky. The warmth of the day had started to cool, and she put her hands on her bare arms and rubbed them up and down. "It's beautiful up here, isn't it?"

Gus took the seat beside hers and sighed. "I could get used to it."

"At least until the snow starts flying in September and lasts until May."

"I wouldn't mind that so much. I've always wanted to go ice fishing." He laid his head back on the chair. "I don't mind the cold. Or snow. Or ice."

"Then life up here would suit you." She peered at him. "Are you thinking of moving up here?"

He shook his head. "Right now, I'm keeping all my options open."

She studied him as he closed his eyes and breathed the smoke-scented air in deeply. He opened his eyes and turned to look at her. "So, what about you? What are your plans?"

"Taking care of Pops."

"And after that?"

She hesitated since she didn't want to think about what would happen after Pops was gone. Since she lived in his house, she'd probably have to sell it and find somewhere else to live. She'd have to clean it out first from over fifty years of accumulated possessions. They were treasures to Pops, but would someone else think her grandmother's hand-crocheted doilies had any value?

"I don't know. To be honest, I try not to think about it."

"But it's coming."

"So you keep telling me."

Gus took a beat. "I'm not trying to fight with you, Cecily. I'm only stating facts. Whether you want to face them or not, certain events will happen."

Cec felt her jaw tighten as she stared into the flames. "Change of topic, please."

They fell silent as the burning wood popped and hissed, sending sparks into the night. Finally, Gus said, "Do you mind if I ask what happened with your divorce?"

She gave a laugh at this. "Why would you want to talk about that?"

"Because you never do. And I'm curious."

"Why?"

Gus gave a shrug. "I thought you said we were becoming friends. Friends share things about their failed marriages."

"Fine. I'll talk about mine if you talk about yours."

She looked at him, expecting him to back down but he agreed instead. "That's fair. What do you want to know?"

A million questions filled her mind, but

the one that she asked was, "How did you get over your divorces?"

"Ahh. You assume that I have."

"You've moved on, haven't you?"

"You seem to have too. But how much of it is just for appearances?"

She bit her lip and tried to find the right words to attach to her feelings. "Sometimes, I think all I did was accept Tom's decision to end the marriage. Because why fight what he had already determined for the both of us?"

"You didn't want to try again?"

She shook her head. "He said he didn't love me anymore. What was I supposed to do? Fight for something he didn't feel? Or that didn't exist?"

It was Gus's turn to fall silent as he stared into the flames. "When Ellie said she was leaving me, I think I was too stunned to fight. I certainly didn't see it coming."

"Ellie was…"

He looked up at her. "My first wife." He gave a smile. "I knew the moment I met her in tenth-grade chemistry that she was the one for me. Evidently, it was the same for her."

"What happened?"

"We got married right after I finished basic training since the army was shipping me to Germany for two years. I mean, we talked about trying it long distance, but she insisted that she'd go with me." He stood, picked up a stick and stabbed at the burning logs. "I don't think she really understood what it meant to be a military spouse." He gave a grunt. "I certainly didn't. I was eighteen and barely knew what it meant to be married, much less what was expected of her."

"But you had each other, so that must have helped."

He gave another poke of the wood so that the tall tower he'd created settled into glowing embers. "We've got the perfect fire for marshmallows now. Should we find some sticks to use?"

They searched the nearby woods and brought back slender branches, which Gus trimmed with his pocket knife. He handed her one, and she opened the bag of marshmallows and placed one at the end of the branch before handing him one. He accepted it, and they sat, holding the marshmallows over the fire, waiting for them to caramelize and soften.

"So what happened that changed things?"

Gus looked at her as if he'd forgotten his story about his first marriage. "Oh, that. After two years in Germany, they moved us back to the states, to Virginia. And I thought everything was okay until I got my deployment orders." He winced. "Afghanistan. When I told Ellie, she said she was moving back to our hometown in Missouri. I assumed she meant she would stay with family while I was fighting overseas, but I guess she'd been planning on leaving, or at least leaving me, for a while before that."

"She broke up with you while you were shipping out? That seems pretty harsh."

"She didn't know I was shipping out when she made her plans. It was just bad timing."

"You're defending her, after all that?" She moved her marshmallow closer to the fire. "Do you still love her?"

He brought his burnt marshmallow out of the fire and blew on it. "Looks like I got too close to the flames." He removed the sticky treat and popped it into his mouth.

"You didn't answer my question."

He put a new marshmallow on the end of his stick. "Do you still love your ex-husband?" he asked without looking at her.

She considered his question. "When I married him I thought I'd love him forever. But can I keep loving someone who doesn't love me back?"

Gus finally turned to look at her and raised a brow. "In a way, you remind me of her. All the rules."

"And did your flouting of the rules annoy her as much as it does me?"

He grinned wide and nodded. "She's a teacher too. Third grade." His smile faded. "She got married again a few years ago. My sister, who still lives in our hometown, told me that she's expecting their first child." He sniffed. "But to answer your question. Yes, she was the love of my life, and part of me will always love her."

He nodded toward her marshmallow. "Looks like it's done."

She carefully drew back her marshmallow from the pit. She left the stick on the table as she took out a graham cracker and placed the melted marshmallow on it before unwrapping a peanut butter cup and placing it over the goo and sandwiching it with another cracker. "I'm not sure about this, but here goes nothing."

She bit into the sweet gooeyness and nodded. "It's gooooood. Different, but still good. Maybe even better." She took another bite.

Once Gus's marshmallow had turned golden, he made himself a s'more. "I'm surprised that a rule follower like you would like something different."

"Sometimes you have to do what is different in order to make things work."

"Good advice to remember." He sampled the s'more and groaned. "I think this is now my favorite way to make s'mores." He finished eating, then looked at her. "Okay. I spilled. Your turn."

"Where to start? I met Tom right before I graduated from college. He was in finance. I was in education, so our paths had never crossed before. One night, a friend of mine invited me to go on a blind date with her boyfriend's roommate."

"Tom?"

"No. Tom was our waiter at the restaurant

that night." She gave a shrug, then smiled at the memory. "I remember I excused myself to go to the bathroom at one point, and Tom approached me. Told me I was out with the wrong man that night. That I should go out with him instead."

"Bold tactic."

"Well, it worked. We went out the next night, and that was it. At least for me. I was head over heels. Until last Christmas when he told me he wasn't in love with me anymore and that I should move out of his house by New Year's."

Gus winced. "Ouch."

"So, I moved in with my friend Vivi until Pops fell and needed me."

"And that's the end of your story?"

Cec thought over his words. "The part with Tom in it. Why would I pine over someone who doesn't want me? Aren't I worth more than that?"

"You are."

She noticed Gus staring intently at her. "You're right. I am. But it hasn't been easy."

"Divorce never is. And I did it twice."

"What happened with your second wife?"

Gus reached for a marshmallow and

placed it on his stick. "That is a story for another campfire."

They stayed out a little longer, making more s'mores for each of them. Eventually, Cec let out a long yawn. She covered her mouth, blinked her eyes a few times. "We should call it a night since we're going to the beach tomorrow."

Gus nodded and looked at the fire. "I'll take care of this if you want to go in and get ready for bed first."

They both stood at the same time, and Cec paused as the glowing campfire sent shadows across his face. He reached over with his thumb and wiped one corner of her mouth. "You've got a little chocolate there."

Her tongue darted to where his thumb had just touched her as her heart pounded in her chest. "Thanks."

"Good night, Cec."

He leaned down and kissed her cheek. She closed her eyes, parting her lips, wishing...things she shouldn't be wishing. She cleared her throat. "Good night, Gus." She started to walk away, then turned to look at him. "Thank you for opening up to me about Ellie."

"Did it help to learn a little more about me?"

If anything, it confused her even more. But she gave him a smile, then walked back to the cabin.

CHAPTER TEN

GUS POURED A cup of coffee for Burt and then one for himself. He brought both to the kitchen island where Burt sat on a stool. Gus came around and took a seat on the stool beside the older man. "How did you sleep?" he asked.

Burt grunted, shrugged and took a long pull of coffee. "You'd think with all this fresh air and activity I'd sleep better. You?"

After the campfire last night, Gus had tossed and turned for hours until falling into a fitful sleep that didn't last. He'd woken up before the sun and rather than continuing to toss and turn, he'd risen and made coffee. "Okay, I guess."

"Which means you didn't."

They fell silent as they watched the sun rise over the lake. Gus studied Burt. "You look like you've got something on your mind. What's going on?"

"These last couple of days with Phyllis have gotten me thinking."

"About?"

"I loved my wife, don't get me wrong. Gladys was the best wife I could have asked for. But seeing Phyllis makes me wonder what would have happened if I had stayed here instead."

"You can't rewrite history. You know that. The choices you made then have turned you into the man you are now."

Burt nodded. "But that doesn't stop the wondering. Thinking about the what-ifs."

Gus thought back to his conversation the night before with Cecily. He'd never meant to share so much about Ellie, but it was like once he started talking about her, he couldn't stop the words. He'd done his fair share of wondering about all the what-ifs with his first wife. What if he had fought for her even as he was away fighting a war? What if he had pursued her once he'd returned home rather than licking his wounds and trying to move on? "I know what you mean."

"But if I hadn't met Glad, I wouldn't have had my son and then Cecily and her brother wouldn't be here."

"And that would be a shame."

Burt grinned at his words. "Mmm-hmm. I'm sure you'd be disappointed."

Gus realized Burt was now watching him with a speculative gleam in his eyes. "What is that supposed to mean?"

"I got up to get a glass of water last night, and I saw you both by the firepit."

"We were talking. And making s'mores."

"Uh-huh. And that kiss you shared?"

Gus frowned, trying to rerun the events of last night through his head. "We didn't kiss."

"So, you're saying that I imagined seeing you lean in and kiss my granddaughter? Son, I may be dying, but I'm not there yet."

Gus felt his cheeks warm as he remembered that moment of an almost kiss. "I kissed her on the cheek when I said good night. That's all it was."

"Uh-huh."

Gus had wanted to kiss her. Could see that she would have welcomed it even, but it hadn't seemed right. Not after talking about their exes, their thoughts on them and not each other. If he kissed Cecily, it would be because she was in his head.

He meant *when* he kissed her. It seemed

inevitable, this pull toward each other. And she seemed to want him like he wanted her. Realizing that Burt was still watching him, Gus cleared his throat. "So, we're spending the day with Phyllis and her family. That should be interesting."

"I guess they make a big deal out of the holiday. A picnic. Swimming. Beach volleyball. And then fireworks at the end of the evening." Burt smiled. "Phyllis always loved the Fourth of July. More than Christmas or any other holiday."

"And she fostered that in her family, obviously."

Gus glanced toward the stairs as Cecily walked down and joined them. She yawned and leaned against the island. "Please tell me you have more coffee ready."

Gus stood and went to the coffee maker to pour her a mug full, added cream and sugar, then handed it to her. She thanked him before she cupped her hands around the mug and took a long drink. "I'm going to need a lot more to get through today."

"Didn't sleep well, baby girl?" Burt asked her.

She glanced at Gus before looking away

and shaking her head. "I think I tossed and turned all night."

"Must be something in the air," Gus muttered, then moved to make another pot of coffee. When he had finished, he turned to see Burt and Cecily staring at him. He pointed to the older man. "Burt said he had trouble sleeping too."

Burt narrowed his eyes at Gus, then nodded. "I did."

Gus eyed Cecily, who watched him for a moment before placing her mug on the island. "Does anyone mind if I take the first shower? I can still smell campfire smoke on my skin and in my hair."

Gus gestured toward the bathroom. "It's all yours."

Cecily smiled, then went back upstairs. Gus watched her leave, then found Burt in turn watching him again. "Does she know?" the older man asked him.

"Does she know what?"

"That you're interested in her."

Gus glanced to the ceiling, then shook his head. "Burt, you know my romantic history. I am not the right man for your granddaughter."

"I know what I see, and that you're a good man who has been searching for the right woman." Burt gave a shrug. "And I think the right woman is right in front of your nose, if you'd take the risk."

"I think seeing Phyllis again has made you turn into a poet. You're seeing romance everywhere."

"Maybe." He picked up his coffee mug from the island and took a quick sip. "Or maybe I'm just hoping that my best friend and my granddaughter might realize the chance at love they're being given."

RELATIVES AND FRIENDS of Phyllis seemed to fill the shoreline by the time the sun was high in the summer sky. Cec applied more sunscreen over Pops's arms, then added a dollop on his nose. "Now rub it in good. The last thing we need is for you to get a sunburn."

"Don't worry. My plan is to find a nice shady spot and plant myself in it." But he rubbed the lotion into his face. "Thank you for taking such good care of me."

Cec spotted a woman approaching them. "If you ask me, I think someone else is looking to take over my job." She greeted Phyllis. "Thank you for inviting us to join you and your family today."

"Of course. What's a few more people when we already have about thirty of us here?" She turned to Pops. "Burt, would you mind coming with me? I have a few folks I'd like to introduce you to."

Pops walked off with Phyllis, who intertwined her arm with his. Cec watched them leave for a moment, then noticed Gus observing her. "What?"

"He's going to be fine."

"I'm sure he is, but I can't help it if I worry. And shouldn't we be included in the people she wants to introduce him to?"

"I say we spend the day not worrying about Burt and find something a lot more fun to do." He looked around the beach. "Want to play some volleyball?"

"They look like they're already in the middle of a game."

"Swimming then?"

She shook her head, knowing she was pouting. It seemed like ever since they'd come to Lighthouse Bay, all Pops wanted to do was spend time with Phyllis. Which was nice for him, but it had her feeling a little left out. Pushed aside.

Gus strode forward and slipped an arm around her shoulders. "Come on. Let's go for a walk at least."

They strolled for a while along the shore, the waves coming in and splashing their feet. Despite the heat of the day, the water was still cool, and Cec squealed the first time the cold wave hit her bare skin.

Farther down the shore, a large lighthouse stood as sentinel over the activities on the beach. Cec shielded her eyes from the sun, then pointed toward the building. "Think the lighthouse is open for tours on the holiday?"

"I don't know. Let's keep going and find out."

The sand turned to pebbles and then rock as they started to climb toward the lighthouse. A sign announced that the structure had been built in 1833 and was responsible for the name of the nearby town. It was now unmanned and automated, but open to the public to explore. Gus grabbed Cec's hand and tugged her forward. "Come on. This should be interesting."

The door opened with ease into a long room with a staircase that led to the upper floors of the lighthouse. Gus stepped aside to let another couple pass them, then they started to climb the spiral stairs to the top. Once there, Gus opened a door to a small platform outside and stepped back to allow Cec to precede him. From there, they could see for miles in the distance across Lake Superior into Canada and beyond.

Gus pointed to cliffs farther down the shore. "My friend Alex said there's a place nearby where you can dive off those cliffs into the lake. What do you think?"

Cec looked skeptical. "As in, do I think I'd want to do that?" She winced. "I'd need to have a death wish to want to jump off a high cliff into a shallow lake. That's a recipe for certain injury, if not worse."

"Alex says it's perfectly safe."

"Thanks, but no. I'll pass."

Gus folded his arms over his chest and leaned casually against the wrought-iron railing. "That's a shocker. You're not much of a risk-taker."

"And you seem to charge toward danger without thinking about the consequences."

"I think about them, but then I choose to take a chance anyway. Then there are other times when you need to do first and think second."

"I've never found that to be the case." She leaned beside him, her bare arm brushing against his. "You must think I'm a real stick-in-the-mud."

"Overly cautious, maybe. But that's one of the things I like about you." He nudged her with his arm. "Now isn't this better than being introduced to a bunch of people we'll probably only see once in our lives and whose names we'll struggle to remember?"

"There's no way Pops could have done those stairs."

"True. But then that means you're stuck with me again."

"I don't mind being stuck with you."

A breeze blew, sending her hair in every direction before she reached up to try to tame it. She knew she should have put it up in a ponytail, but she'd chosen to wear it down instead that morning.

Gus reached over and pushed a stray hair behind her ear. She looked at him, remembering that moment by the campfire last night. Gus's tongue darted out to wet his lips, then he started to lean in toward her. She let her eyes drift shut.

"Oh, excuse us. We didn't know anyone else was up here," a woman said, interrupting the moment. "Wow. This is a great view, isn't it?"

Gus smiled at her, then led Cec around the deck to give the couple some space to check out the shoreline. But he didn't make a move to kiss her again.

THE SKY DARKENED as the sun set. Cecily sat on the ground at Burt's feet, and Gus next to her. It had been a fun day, but long. After leaving the lighthouse, they had returned to the beach and played a couple games of very competitive volleyball with Phyllis's family. Gus reached up and rubbed his shoulder, which was sore after he'd banged into Cecily when they both had gone after the ball and crashed into each other instead. Then they'd had a feast of barbecue and enough sides to fill an entire table with food. And then another table full of desserts. He'd eaten two plates' worth of sweets.

He smiled and then leaned back on an elbow to stare out at the night sky. There had been clouds earlier that threatened rain, but they seemed to have held off until after the upcoming fireworks. It would be the perfect ending to a perfect day.

"Oh shoot." Burt fiddled with the oxygen tank beside him. "I think it's run out."

Cecily turned to look at him. "We have another backup in the car, right? I'll go get it."

Gus sat up and waved her back down. "It's fine. You stay here, and I'll run and get it really quickly."

"You don't think I can get there faster than you? I might be tiny, but I'm swift on my feet."

"I wasn't commenting on your speed, Cecily. But you should stay here with Burt and enjoy the fireworks. I'll be fine."

He stood and set the backpack air condenser on Burt's lap before unscrewing the air hose from the empty tank. "I know the battery is running low but use this in the meantime. I'll be right back."

He reached down and hefted the empty tank into his arms and strode toward the parking lot. He had just reached the rental SUV when he heard the slap of sandals on the pavement behind him. He turned to find Cecily running toward him. "You didn't have to come. I told you I had it."

"The hose is getting kinked up and twisted, so I thought I'd get a new one."

"Oh. Good idea."

Suddenly, there was the sound of a rocket being sent into the air and then the explosion of color and sound. Cecily turned her face to the sky and smiled. "The fireworks are starting."

Gus watched her instead of the fireworks as the different colors reflected on her face. She oohed and aahed as each new rocket exploded in the sky. She turned to find him still watching her. "You're missing it."

"No, I'm not."

He took a step toward her, then put his hands on her hips, tugging her closer to him. Her eyes widened before drifting closed as he lowered his mouth to hers. He placed a soft kiss against her lips, then started to back away, wondering what in the world he was thinking. But Cecily followed his mouth and pressed herself to him. He moaned and pulled her even closer, pushing one hand into the back of her hair while the other anchored her to him.

What was meant to be a taste turned into an exploration. One he'd never forget.

A series of explosions filled the air, and Gus stepped away from Cecily, his breath ragged and heart beating as if he'd been running a marathon. Realizing he wanted her in his arms again, he moved forward, but Cecily placed a hand on his chest. "The battery is running low, remember? And I don't think we should go any further." She closed her eyes for a split second and caught his gaze when she'd opened them again. "If you'll carry the tank, I've got the tubing."

As she walked on, he wondered if he could undo what he'd done wrong.

CHAPTER ELEVEN

CEC STARED UP at the ceiling of the bedroom, trying to sleep. In the distance, she could hear revelers still setting off fireworks and celebrating the Fourth. But it wasn't the noise keeping her awake.

What in the world had she been thinking when she'd kissed Gus? True, they'd had several misses before, but it had happened. Finally. And while she was kissing him, she had felt like everything had clicked into place. But once they stopped kissing, reality had returned and made her aware that this was a man who would be leaving once he found his next adventure. He'd be leaving Thora for good. And leaving her as well.

The idea of getting involved with Gus was wrong on several levels. Besides him leaving town, he didn't appreciate the rules, any rules for that matter. He followed his own whims and flitted wherever the wind took him. He'd admitted that he didn't do relationships.

The other side of her brain reminded her that it had only been kissing. He hadn't made any declarations or promises. It had been a moment between two consenting adults, and the moment had passed.

So why was she replaying the kiss over and over in her mind? Why was she struggling to stay in her bed rather than walk to the room next door and ask him what was happening between them? Because something was. She didn't know what it was, couldn't define it, but there was certainly something going on between them.

Temporary. That's all she was to him. And the strain of taking care of Pops must be getting to her because she wanted to throw caution to the wind. If it lasted two days or two weeks or two years, did it really matter? If anything, Pops's condition reminded her that life was short. And why shouldn't she try to hold on to a little bit of happiness with everything she had?

She rolled onto her belly and buried her head into her pillow. Ruminating about

Gus and trying to figure out what was in his head wasn't helping her relax enough to fall asleep. She sighed. She could really use a good, long conversation with Vivi.

A knock on her door brought her sitting up. "Yes?"

The door opened, and Gus stood there. "Do you have a minute?"

She reached over and turned the small light on beside the bed. "Everything okay with you?"

He took a seat at the end of the bed and ran a hand through his hair. "It's fine. I just… I wanted to make sure you were okay."

She straightened and stared at him. "Why wouldn't I be?"

"Because we kissed."

She gave a nod. "I know. I was there."

"Right. But we're still cool, the two of us?"

"Of course we are."

Gus nodded. "Good. I was worried that it would change something between us."

She tried to keep the disappointment out of her voice. Well, that answered that question in her mind. "Everything's fine." Her cell phone rang, and she glanced at the screen. Vivi. She held up the phone. "I should take this."

"Well, good night then."

She called good night to him then answered the phone. "Girl, you've got great timing."

"Uh-oh. That sounds ominous." Vivi chuckled.

"More like I really needed to talk to you." She settled back into the bed after turning out the bedside lamp. She stared into the darkness. "He thought that kiss had been nothing? That it hadn't changed anything? So why did it change something inside me?"

"Whoa. You've got to back up a little and fill some details in for me. Who kissed you? Not Gus."

Cec told her about how things had developed between her and Gus. And how the kiss earlier that evening had affected her. Gus was the first man she'd kissed since Tom, and that had to mean something, didn't it?

"Of course it does. You've allowed yourself to picture a different future with someone new. And maybe that someone is Gus."

"Or not, since he doesn't seem interested. Which is fine since I don't think things would work out with us anyways."

Vivi huffed on the other end. "I wish I could be there in person right now."

"I wish that too." They hung up with promises to get together once Cec got back to town.

Cec went back to staring at the ceiling. She knew Gus was right. Nothing should change between them. After all, he was planning on leaving town for good, while she had every intention of staying.

So why did she feel like she was losing something she had just found?

The knock on the bedroom door woke up Gus from a nice dream he'd been having. Cecily opened the door. "Gus, I need you. It's Pops." She turned on her heel and left the room.

Gus pulled on a pair of jeans, grabbed his medical bag and ran down the stairs barefoot. Burt looked up from where he sat on the sofa. The color in his face was gray, his lips blue. "Is the oxygen tank plugged in?"

Cecily nodded. "Yes. It's the first thing I checked."

"I'm fine." Pops tried to shoo them away. Gus and Cecily stayed put.

Burt ran a hand around the back of his neck. "I feel...tired...but I'm...fine."

"You're blue. You're not fine." Cecily pointed at Gus, who took a seat next to Burt. "Check him out. Do what you have to do, but find out what's wrong."

Gus took out the stethoscope and had Burt take a few deep breaths. His lungs sounded clear for the most part, and his heartbeat was strong and steady. He then took Burt's temperature and checked his blood pressure. "His temperature is a little high, but everything else is normal."

Cecily frowned and took a seat next to Burt. "What could cause the fever?"

"It could be an infection that he's fighting. A cold. Or it could be nothing."

Burt frowned. "Don't talk...like I'm not...sitting right here." He turned to his granddaughter and took a deep breath. "I told you... I'm tired...but I'm okay. I need... to take it a little...easier today. That's all."

"Pops, you need to take it all the way easy." Cecily sighed. "While we need to cancel our plans for today."

Burt shook his head. "No. My old house."

"You heard Gus. You've got an elevated temp, which could be nothing or it could be an infection, either way, right now you need to get some rest."

Gus put a hand on Burt's shoulder. "I know you've been looking forward to it since we decided to come here. But I don't think it's a good idea today. You should take it easy, and we can go see your old house tomorrow."

"Time is...running out."

Cecily put her arms around Burt. "Pops, if you push yourself too hard, you're only going to get sicker. And we'll be going home earlier than you want to. Take today and rest. We'll go sightseeing tomorrow."

Burt shook his head. "My plans? Phyllis?"

"Tell her you need to rest. She'll understand that your plans are only delayed until tomorrow." Cecily laid her head on his shoulder. "It's just one day, Pops. And if you agree to rest until tonight, maybe we can make plans to meet Phyllis for dinner. How does that sound?"

"I want to see her."

"You'll have to settle for talking to her for now." She handed him his cell phone. "Gus and I can step outside to give you some privacy."

They walked out onto the deck, and Gus said, "His temperature is probably nothing."

Cecily nodded, but she didn't seem convinced. "Still, a fever is not a good sign. Even I know that."

"We've been pushing hard every day for the last week, so I think you're right. Let him sleep and do nothing until tonight, then we'll reevaluate."

"Is that your medical advice?"

"It is." Gus looked over at her. "Since our plans are on hold, would you mind if I left the two of you for a bit to go see my friend Alex at his resort? He mentioned wanting to talk to me about something."

"Of course."

THE DRIVE UP to the resort only magnified the beauty of the place. The trees with the blue skies beyond and the lake in the background. Even the timber that made up the lodge looked majestic. Gus found Alex in the office where the front desk receptionist had told him he'd be. He knocked on the door, and Alex glanced away from his computer. He smiled and waved him in. "I wasn't expecting you today."

"Is this a bad time?"

"Are you kidding me? This is perfect." Alex stood and approached Gus. "I want to show you something. Follow me."

Gus followed him down the hall to a room that he unlocked with one of several keys on a large keychain. They stepped inside, and Alex turned on the light revealing a small room that looked like a mini clinic. Alex turned to Gus. "What do you think?"

Gus took a guess. "It's a first aid room?"

Alex smiled and pointed at Gus. "And I want to hire you to staff it. Along with performing some other duties like being a guide for hiking, hunting, fishing, you name it. What do you think?"

Gus thought he must have missed something. "Are you offering me a job?"

"The guy who used to staff our on-site triage quit last month, and I've been trying to find a replacement. Then you walk into the bar the other night, and I figured that this must be fate. I need someone with medical experience to take care of my guests, until they can get to a doctor or hospital if that's what's needed, and you mention you're looking for a new job. Fate."

"I'm looking to get away from the medical field, not be in the middle of it again."

"Your duties around here would be more as a guide than a medic. But I do need someone with medical experience, which you have. And someone who loves the outdoors, like you do. It's a perfect fit."

"I don't know."

"We have several cabins on the property that are empty. You could move into one of those. I could have you on staff by the end of the month."

"I..." Part of him was intrigued by the offer. He could still use his medical background, but he'd have more freedom and space than he had in his prior jobs. And it wasn't like he had a bunch of offers being thrown at him. "What would the salary be like if I came to work for you?"

Alex named a figure that was substantially below what he'd made as a paramedic. "But you'd have the cabin included, along with all your meals here at the resort.

Plus, the cost of living isn't nearly as expensive as it is where you live currently."

"I'll have to think this over."

Alex nodded. "That's all I'm asking. But I think this would be ideal for you."

CEC GLANCED OUT the window, thinking she would see the rented SUV pull into the driveway any minute. "Expecting someone?"

She turned to find Pops watching her from the sofa. "I thought Gus would be back by now. Didn't you?"

Pops smiled knowingly. "He's seeing a friend. They've probably got to talking and lost track of time."

"It's not like he told me when he'd be back, but..." She glanced at her watch. "It's been half the day. What if..." She let her words drop, but her thoughts continued. What if he had finally found the place he was supposed to be? What if his next adventure was here?

She stopped herself. What would it matter if it was? It's not like they had any commitment. They had shared one kiss. One. That didn't mate them for life, for goodness' sake. She reached up and took the tie out of her ponytail and shook her hair loose, then turned to Pops. "We probably shouldn't plan on him making it back in time for dinner, so what would you like to do? We don't have a car, but I could order some food and have it delivered."

"Why are you changing the subject? Is something wrong?"

"Nothing is wrong." But he kept looking at her, so she sighed. "Fine. You know how I get when my plans are upended. And today has definitely changed to something we didn't expect." She peered at him more closely. "By the way, your color's a lot better." She placed a hand against his forehead. "And your fever is down. That's good. How are you feeling?"

He swatted her hand away. "Much better. I guess I did need some rest like you suggested."

"I don't do things to hurt you, but to help you."

"I know." He took her hand in his. "Which is why I think you and I need to have a talk. Because we seem to have been avoiding this one, and it's not meant to hurt you but to help."

She didn't like the sound of that. He took several deep breaths, closing his eyes. "Pops, what is it? Are you in pain?"

He opened his eyes and looked at her. "I know my time is getting short."

She shook her head. "No."

She started to stand, but he took a hold of her hand and tugged her back down to the sofa. "Please. We need to talk about this."

"I can't."

"But we have to, Cecily Joyce."

She blinked at his use of her full name. He only used it when he was serious, so she finally took the seat beside him.

"Back home, I have a folder in the nightstand by my bed where you'll find my last wishes written down. I don't want a funeral or a viewing. You can have a huge party for my send-off, but I don't want a bunch of crying, and no one is allowed to wear black."

"Pops…"

"I mean it. I've led a very good life, and I've enjoyed more time than most get, so you're to have a celebration of my life. Understood?"

"Yes, but…"

"No buts. This is what I want. In the folder, you'll find some possible venues, along with price lists and my recommendations for the menu. I also made a playlist of some of my favorite songs."

"You've really thought it all out."

"I've had the time to think about it, so yes. Since I know how you are about your lists, there's plenty of them. Who is to be notified. Where I want my obituary published, which I've also started to write."

It seemed so macabre to be sitting inside on a beautiful sunny day talking about this. But she nodded as he continued to tell her his plans for the end of his life. He didn't seem sad as he talked, but straightforward and matter-of-fact. On the other hand, she wanted to cry and scream and run away. She looked down at her hands, which she had gripped tightly together in her lap. She let them go and shook them out.

"Do you understand what I'm saying, baby girl?"

She looked up at him and nodded. "You're

trying to make it easier on me once you're gone. But it's not going to be easy. Yes, you've lived longer than most, including Granny, but that won't make me miss you any less." A tear escaped, and she got angry at herself for allowing it. She reached up and wiped it away. "Lists won't help me grieve you."

"But they will. You'll see in time."

"Pops, maybe when we get back home we can talk to your doctor. There are break-throughs in medicine all the time. Maybe there's something that we missed. Some-thing they could do now to help you."

"There's nothing more they can do. And I don't want them to. I've lived my life."

"But I don't want you to die!"

Pops gave a soft nod. "I know. Which brings me to the next hard thing I have to say." He took another deep breath. "I don't want you to give up on your dreams."

She frowned, trying to figure out what he was talking about. "What dreams have I given up on?"

"Love, for one."

"I haven't…"

"I know that Tom hurt you and putting

yourself out there again will probably bring you more hurt, but you shouldn't close yourself off to love happening again." He scooted closer to her. "When Gladys died, it felt like part of my heart died with her. But these last few days with Phyllis showed me that it didn't die. It only fell asleep. And now it's waking up, and…" He reached over and put a hand on her shoulder. "I don't want you to miss out on the dream of being in love again. Especially when there is a good man right in front of you."

"You're talking about Gus?" She gave a laugh, then sobered when she realized that's who Pops meant. "I'm not in love with him."

"Because you won't allow yourself to be."

"Because chances are he's going to leave Thora." *And me.* "He's not planning on staying around. Why would I open up my heart to someone who is planning on going?"

"He could be convinced to stay. If you gave him the right reason to."

She shook her head. "Pops, you can write out lists for me to follow after you're gone, and I promise that I'll do just that to the letter. But you can't write a love story between me and Gus. He'll never stay. And I'll never leave. So that is one dream that will never happen."

"I just don't want you to give up on the dream of someone new. Don't be like me and wait until it's too late to see if something could happen."

GUS FOUND CEC sitting by the firepit when he returned late that night. She had lit a smaller campfire than they had enjoyed before, and she sat on one of the Adirondack chairs wrapped in a quilt, staring into the flames. He took a seat in the chair next to hers. "Hey."

She turned to look at him. "You're back."

"I didn't plan on being gone this long. Is Burt doing okay?"

He'd checked in on the older man who was sleeping on the sofa before coming outside. His color looked better, and he hadn't felt warm to the touch. Cec nodded. "You were right about it being something small. I guess I tend to overreact when it comes to him."

"It's understandable."

They fell silent as they watched the

campfire. Gus moved some of the logs so that the embers glowed. "Did I miss anything today?"

"Did you know that Pops has planned out everything he wants to happen after he's gone? And we're not allowed to have a funeral for him?" She glanced over at him, and Gus noticed that her eyes were rimmed in red. "It's like he's accepted this. There's no fight left in him."

"Because he's at peace with what is going to happen."

"Well, I'm not." She reached up and wiped under one eye. "And that probably makes me very selfish, but I'm angry."

"At Burt?"

"Yes. At him. At the cancer. At the world. At everything."

"At me?" he asked softly.

She swiped another tear away. "Why would I be mad at you?"

"If you're not now, you will be after I tell you what happened today."

She looked shocked and he thought about postponing his announcement. From the sounds of it, she'd had a rough day, and he didn't want to add on to it. But holding off on the truth didn't seem right, either. "I got a job offer at my friend's resort."

He told her about the details, and as he did so, he could feel the excitement building within him for this job opportunity. It could be the right fit for him. It could be his next adventure.

"You accepted the job?"

"Not yet."

She sniffed. "But you will. It's a great chance, and it's beautiful up here. You'd be happy."

"Alex would want me to start by the end of this month."

"So soon?"

"It's one possibility that I have."

"What's the other?"

He looked at her. "Staying in Thora. At least for now until…" He sighed. "I don't want to leave Burt before he dies. You're going to need my help, especially as we get closer to the end."

"I'll be fine. We can hire nurses to help me and my mom. Maybe you shouldn't let this chance go."

"I'm offering more than just the use of my medical skills, Cec. I'm a friend. To you both. I can be a strong shoulder to lean on when things get tough. So, if you wanted me to, I could wait and start at the resort after..."

"Are you asking me if I want you to stay?"

He supposed that he was. With Ellie, he hadn't asked her what she wanted. He had assumed that his plans were also hers. But he'd soon learned that they had been on different paths. "Would you want me to?"

CHAPTER TWELVE

THE HOUSE STOOD back from the road, a large oak tree in the front yard blocking most of it from view. Cec crossed her arms as she stared up at it. Apparently abandoned for years, it looked in disrepair, windows cracked, roof covered in old leaves and broken tree branches. Parts of the aluminum siding were missing, and one of the gutters hung down, no longer attached to the house. Pops sighed beside her. "It didn't look like this when I lived here. Granddad built it from wood, so another owner must have added all the siding."

Cec was worried, naturally. "I don't think we should risk going inside. It could be dangerous if it's been sitting empty for a long while."

Gus strode toward the front porch and walked up the two steps, which groaned in protest. "How about I take a quick look around and see if it's safe?"

Pops waved off their hesitations. "It will be fine. My granddad built this house to last."

"If it were maintained, I'm sure it would. But this doesn't look promising." She figured critters might be the current residents of the house, and she wasn't that fond of mice or creepy crawlies.

"I want to see the inside. I didn't come all this way just to turn around."

Gus looked at them from the porch's top step. "And what was going to be your plan if someone lived here?"

Cec jumped in. "Actually, I researched it before we left this morning and discovered it was empty. The last owner died without heirs a few years ago, so it's been unoccupied while lawyers and the state decide what to do with it." She propped her hands on her hips. "But I still don't like this. We'd be trespassing if we go inside."

Gus checked the front door, and the knob turned. "But if the door was left open…" He looked at Cec, then shrugged before entering. "Here goes nothing."

Pops walked up the steps next and followed Gus inside. Cec glanced around to see if anyone could see them sneaking into the house, but the nearest neighbor was far down the street. She took a deep breath, then followed the two men inside.

The interior of the home smelled musty with disuse. The walls appeared to be caked in dust and grime. Skittering sounds from the upstairs seemed to indicate where the mice lived. "I still don't know about this," Cec said again. "It doesn't feel right to be poking around here."

Pops walked through the living room into the kitchen at the back of the house. He sighed and ran a hand along one of the counters. "It's been updated since I left, but it looks vaguely familiar. As if the lines of my memory have been blurred a little." He pointed to the window that looked onto the backyard. "Mama had the kitchen table there under that window. I would stare outside while I was supposed to be doing my homework while she cooked at the stove." He knocked on the kitchen counter. "She ruled the home from her place right here. Advice and discipline were handed out, along with fresh-baked cookies and kisses and stern warnings when we sassed back."

He glanced at Cec. "I wish you could have met her. She was quite a woman."

Cec linked her arm through Pops's. "I wish I'd had the chance." Oma had died a few months before she had been born, so she had relied on her grandparents' memories of her to color in her mental picture of her great-grandmother.

Pops looked around the kitchen. "This seems so much smaller than I remember. And I definitely don't remember a door being there." He walked over and opened it to reveal a pantry. "We never had a pantry, but we did have a cellar. You had to walk outside to get to it from the side of the house. Mama used it to store all her canning and any food she could preserve. My dad built shelves for her. As many as she needed. He'd grumble when she ran out of room and asked for another shelf, but he built it all the same. And she'd bake his favorite chocolate cake as thanks."

He turned and looked at Gus. "I'd like to see the bedrooms upstairs, but I don't know if I can make it up those stairs alone."

Gus gave a short nod. "I can help you. We'll take it slow."

Pops consented, and Gus put his arm

around his waist, and they ascended the stairs, one at a time. Cec followed, being careful to step around one of the treads that looked like her foot would go through the wood.

Upstairs, there were two bedrooms. Cec wrinkled her nose. "No bathroom up here?"

"We only had the one downstairs off the living room." He pointed to the first room off the hallway. "My brother and I shared this one until I left for the navy."

They walked inside to find a twin mattress lying on the floor between two windows that overlooked the front yard. Pops grinned as he walked to the closet and opened the door. "I wonder if it's still here..."

He disappeared into the closet for a moment, then called out for Gus. "I need a hand."

Gus entered the closet with him and helped Pops lift a floorboard in the corner. Pops crowed and pulled out a small, dusty wooden car from its hiding spot. He handed it to Cec. "My treasures are still here after all these years. I knew it was a good hiding spot."

She looked at the car and noticed the

way Pops's name was scratched on the underside. He then handed her a small coin purse. "Unfortunately, this is empty. But then, growing up, it usually was. I wasn't known for saving any change I got from doing odd jobs around the house. Spent it as quickly as I earned it. My brother Norman on the other hand, could squeeze a dime until it screamed." He sighed and returned to looking into the hiding place before producing a small notebook. "I used to write story ideas down in here."

When he handed it to Cec, she gave the notebook a perusal, finding the tiny, neat handwriting of her grandfather. The ink had started to fade with time. "I didn't know you used to write stories."

Pops shrugged. "I never actually wrote the stories, but I was very good at coming up with ideas."

She flipped through the fragile pages, then smiled as she read a few of the jotted lines. "I should have known. They're mostly ideas about stories with cowboys."

Pops grunted as he stood. "I've always loved Westerns."

She handed the notebook to Gus, who

read through several pages before saying, "Here's one about a heroic cowboy type rescuing the pretty damsel in distress before riding off into the sunset with her. And there's a little note that says to name the heroine Phyllis."

Pops colored then coughed. "That was before I got the nerve to ask her out for the first time. I thought she was the prettiest girl in school. And I guess she seemed to be the perfect muse for that particular tale."

Gus handed Pops the notebook. "I think we should take your treasures with us."

Pops nodded and walked out of the closet. "There's one more thing I want to see, then we can go. It's out in the backyard."

Gus helped Pops once again to navigate the stairs, and they walked out the back door into the huge yard that was bordered by cherry trees. Pops put his hand up and pulled down a few pieces of the ripe fruit. "Mama made the best pies from these." He popped a cherry into his mouth before Cec could protest. "Mmm, just as tart as I remember."

He walked to one of the trees and put a hand on the trunk. "Here it is."

Carved into the wood was "BK + PL" surrounded by a lopsided heart. "I thought my dad wouldn't stop hollering when he found out I had done this. Said it would kill the tree." He reached up and pulled another cherry off. "Looks like it survived just fine."

"You really loved her all those years ago." Cec put an arm around his shoulders.

"I did." He smiled back at her. "Which reminds me. We should get going. I'm supposed to meet with her this afternoon to make up for our missed date yesterday."

A squawk from a walkie-talkie sounded before a voice called out from behind them, "Folks, I need you to step this way slowly."

Cec turned to find two uniformed cops standing by the house, watching them. "Sorry. My grandfather wanted to see his old childhood home one last time."

One of the officers removed his sunglasses and peered at them. "Well, it no longer belongs to him, so the three of you need to get a move on."

"We didn't mean to trespass," she told them.

Gus gave her a look, since they *had* meant to. She raised a brow at him, then turned back to the cops. "We were just leaving."

One of the cops watched them as if expecting them to make a run for it. Instead, they walked out of the backyard through the side gate and got into the rented SUV. Once they were on the road once more, Gus started laughing. "Can you imagine if they had arrested us? We could have made the front page of the town's newspaper. Former citizen trespasses into his old house. Or gang breaks into abandoned home."

"How about robbers steal car from deserted home?" Cec held up the wooden car that she still had in her hand.

Pops joined in the laughter. "I would have had to call Phyllis to bail us out." He shook his head. "That would have been a great story to tell about me for years."

Gus winked at Cec. "Oh, I'm going to tell it. Maybe with a few embellishments. Like how the cops had their guns drawn while Burt held a bag of loot he'd taken from the house."

Cec could feel her cheeks aching from smiling so much. "You can't tell a story like that about my grandfather. What would people think?"

Pops grinned in the back seat. "Maybe that I had lived a life beyond what they expected."

THE SOUND OF the waterfall crashing into the lake below made Cec pale as she hung on to the trunk of a tree while Gus hiked farther up the trail in front of her. He called out to her. "Come on. Alex said that the perfect place to dive is just up ahead."

She felt her stomach drop and tried to explain. "I never agreed to actually jump off this mountain."

"It's not a mountain, Cec. Don't give in to your fear."

"I'm not afraid."

Gus stopped and cocked his head to one side, and peered at her. She put her arms tighter around the tree. "It's not fear so much as panic. Anxiety."

Gus walked back down the trail toward her. "What are you anxious about?"

Standing at the edge, staring down into the abyss. Jumping and continuing to fall,

fall, fall. Hitting a rock on the way down. Pick one, she wanted to tell him.

But she didn't say any of that. Instead, she pointed back toward the trail. "I remember there was a much better place to jump back where we started."

"You mean safer."

"Lower to the water, yes."

Gus looked at her. "I never knew you were afraid of heights."

"I told you, it's not that I'm afraid, per se."

"Right. You're anxious." He leaned on the tree next to hers. "Alex said the view from there is unlike any other in the Upper Peninsula. It would be a shame to miss it." He held out his hand to her. "How about I walk with you and protect you?"

She glanced at the hand, then gave a small nod. Maybe if she had him to hang on to, her panic wouldn't grow into full-blown terror. "Okay."

They walked hand in hand farther up the trail. Gus glanced over at her, and she turned to look at him. "What?"

He shook his head. "Nothing. Just that the exercise is blooming roses in your cheeks. You've never looked lovelier."

Her hair was up in a messy bun. She was dressed in an old T-shirt advertising a band she'd loved years ago over her bathing suit and cutoff denim shorts. She screwed her face up. "I think we need to get you an appointment with the eye doctor once we get home."

Gus laughed and squeezed her hand, then urged her up the trail a little quicker. "I know what I see, and what I see is a beautiful woman."

"I still think you need to get your eyes checked."

They reached a plateau on the trail, and Gus pointed to a hand-carved wooden sign that read High Dive. "Here it is." He stepped to the edge and gave a whistle, then pulled her closer. "Alex was right. Look at that view."

She opened her eyes, then shut them immediately. "I can't look."

"Open your eyes, Cec, or you're going to miss out on something amazing."

She opened one eye, then quickly shut it. They were up so high, and the ground felt as if it would fall from beneath her. She took a deep breath, then opened both eyes and stared out straight ahead. "It is a beautiful view. You can see Canada from here."

Gus tugged on her hand so that they got to the edge of the waterfall. "So, this is where we jump."

Cec shook her head and backed away from the edge. "No, this is where you jump. I'm going to take the trail back down."

"We can jump together. How about that?"

Her stomach clenched at the thought of letting go from up this high. She removed her hand from Gus's grip. "No, thanks. I can't."

He peered at her for a long moment, looking as if he was going to try to convince her again. But then he gave a quick nod. "Okay then. I'll meet you below at the edge of the lake."

Then he winked at her and jumped off. Cec gasped and peered down to see him break the surface of the water. She waited until she saw his head pop up before she turned and started down the trail.

GUS SAT ON the beach beside the lake while he waited for Cec to find her way back down the trail beside the waterfall. The jump had been amazing. He'd never felt more alive than when he'd let go and allowed gravity to pull him down to earth. Not quite the same rush from skydiving, but it had been close. Then the plunge into the lake and swimming to resurface. Amazing. He was going to have to do that again.

He only wished he could have convinced Cec to jump with him. That would have made it even better. He could understand fear keeping you from doing something. But he also knew that letting something hold you back was no way to live, at least, in his opinion.

Cec was definitely cautious. He got that but hoped she wasn't missing out on life.

She walked up to him and sat down on the sandy ground next to him. "How was the jump?"

He grinned at her. "Remarkable."

"Looked like it."

"We could walk up again, and this time you could jump with me. Come on. What do you say?"

Cec shook her head and leaned back on the sand, resting on her elbows. "I admire you for your reckless abandon—"

"I wouldn't say it was reckless."

"—but I'm not like you."

He looked at her, then leaned back to lay next to her. "I'm not asking you to be like me. I'm only asking that you try something you've never done before."

"I don't need to try everything in order to have a good life."

"I never said that."

"But you seemed to imply it." She shook her head at him. "I have a good life, even if I do follow the rules and plan every little detail out."

"I know you do."

"And you have a good life where you can leave on a whim and jump off a cliff and agree to a job hundreds of miles away."

So that was what this was about? "Cec, I never said I'd take the job with Alex."

"But you're considering it."

"Sure I am. It's a great opportunity. But the timing isn't right for it."

She sat up and pulled her legs up to her chest, wrapping her arms around her knees. "If Pops wasn't a factor, would you be hesitating?"

"He's only one part of this." He looked at her. "So are you."

Her head reared back. "Me?"

Gus sat up and scooted close to her. "Yes, you. When we planned this trip, I never expected that these…feelings would grow. I never intended for anything to happen between us."

She glanced down at the sand. "And what exactly is happening between us?"

"I don't know. But we've been getting along really well, and then we kissed. And it was a pretty good kiss."

"Yes, it was." Her cheeks reddened. "But it was only kissing. Nothing more."

He looked at her. "Wasn't it? I haven't been able to sleep the last couple of nights because I'm trying to figure out what *is* going on with us, and I don't have any answers. I was hoping that maybe you did."

"Sorry. No, I don't have any answers. Just more questions."

He reached over and put a hand on her cheek. "You're not interested in something casual or temporary. I know this, but yet I can't stop myself from wanting you."

"I never said that."

Gus cocked his head to one side. "You're a forever kind of woman, Cec. Unfortunately, that's something I can't offer you."

She looked down at the frayed edges of her shorts and picked at a thread. "I know. But after Tom, maybe I don't need a forever. Maybe I need to have a summer romance to get over him for good. A fling that only lasts for a little while."

Gus shook his head. "No, you don't. I've been where you are, and trust me, I know what I'm talking about. Flings only feel good while they're happening. And when they're over, it's like you go through the heartbreak that had only been on hold, waiting for you to wake up and get back to where you were before. Is that what you want?"

She looked at him. "So, what do we do?"

"I don't know. I'm not going to be sticking around."

"What if you did? What if I did ask you to stay?"

Could he stay in one place for her? Could he stick it out and explore this or would he one day resent the fact that he'd given up on a chance for a different life? "Being on this road trip has really pushed us together.

Fast. Maybe if we spend some time apart, once we're back in Thora, we'll both return to reality. Our feelings will go away."

"You think this is happening only because we've been spending so much time together this past week?"

"Don't you? And then there's all of Burt's talk about romance and grabbing on to love while you get a chance, and what else would we be thinking about but each other?"

She gave a nod but didn't look at him, and he felt as if he'd said the wrong thing. Then she quietly said, "You're right. We should back off from whatever this is."

Although she repeated what he'd just said, he wanted to protest. But instead of that, he sighed. "I'm glad we're on the same page."

Then he wondered if he had just made the biggest mistake of his life.

CEC CHECKED HER phone again. Close to ten o'clock at night and still no word from Pops. Where in the world was he? It wasn't like him to stay out this late. Not that he had a curfew, for goodness' sake, but he was all for early to bed, early to rise. Cec got off the sofa and walked to the front window to stare out into the darkness. Should she call him?

"He's fine. Can you please sit down so we can finish this game?"

She turned to glance at the board of word tiles they'd placed on the coffee table by the sofa. "I'm much better with numbers than words. Want to play that dice game again?" she asked.

He laughed. "You beat me three times. Let me win at least one game."

She sat back down on the floor at the coffee table and glanced at the letters on her wood frame. *S. X. Z. E. I. L. R.* The *X* and *Z* were killing her chances of a victory. She glanced again at her phone. "I can't shake the feeling that something is wrong."

Gus laid down his letters. "Gilded. Triple letter on the *G*. Triple word score." He counted up his points and noted it on the scratch pad between them. "Your turn."

She laid down the *S, L, I,* and *E* building off the *D*. "Slide." She grabbed four more tiles and arranged them on the frame. "The thing is that he would call if he was going to stay out this late. He wouldn't want me to worry."

Gus's expression was full of kindness. "Listen. He's in love again, and he wants to spend as much time with Phyllis as he can while we're here. Can you really blame him?"

"But he could at least call."

"He's over eighty, so he doesn't have to answer to you. Or to me." He laid down another word and smiled, his score far ahead of hers.

"I know he's not a child, but…"

Her phone started to ring. She turned the screen to show Gus that it was Pops. "Finally." She pushed the button to answer. "Hey, Pops. I was just—"

"Cecily, dear, it's Phyllis."

Her stomach dropped, and her breath caught in her chest. "What happened?"

They had been enjoying a late dinner on the deck of Phyllis's house when Pops complained of tightness in his chest and trouble breathing. Phyllis had checked the tank, but it was full and there were no kinks in the tubing. They couldn't find a reason for it. When Pops got to his feet, he collapsed but was conscious. Phyllis had called 911, and they were heading to the hospital now. Could she and Gus meet them there?

Cec closed her eyes. She'd known something was wrong. "Of course. Let me give the phone to Gus so you can give him directions."

She handed him the phone, then got to her feet. She had to find her purse and her shoes. And where was her phone? She glanced at Gus. Right. He had it in his hand.

Once Gus had gotten the information from Phyllis, she already had her shoes on her feet and her purse over her shoulder. Gus handed her the phone, and she looked up at him. "This is it, isn't it? We're at the end."

Gus put his hands on her shoulders. "That's not what it sounds like. This is a setback, but this is not the end."

"Are you sure?"

"Burt is conscious and talking. That's a good sign. Let's focus on that rather than thinking about the worst-case scenario, okay?"

Cec gave a nod and followed him quickly out to the car.

CHAPTER THIRTEEN

At the hospital, they found Phyllis waiting in the emergency room. She stood as they entered. "He's with the doctors right now. Cecily, Burt asked that you join him as soon as you got here."

Cec nodded and walked to the nurses' station. A nurse ushered her back to a private room. Pops sat on a hospital bed hooked up to several machines. The heart monitor beeped regularly, which gave her hope. "Hey, Pops," she said.

Pops opened his eyes. "Baby girl."

She held up a hand. "Don't try to talk right now. Just breathe in that oxygen. We can talk later, okay?"

He nodded and patted the side of the bed. She walked toward him and put her hand in his. She stood by his side, and he closed his eyes once more. She watched him as he rested, clinging to his hand as if it was a lifeline keeping her connected to him. As if she could send good health through the touch of their hands.

The door to the room opened, and a doctor in teal scrubs and a white lab coat entered. He looked up at her from the tablet he was viewing. "You must be the granddaughter. Herbert said to expect you."

"I am." She glanced at Pops. "What's going on with him? Why did he have difficulty breathing? Why did he collapse?"

"We're not quite sure what happened, but we're running some tests to determine what is going on. I understand he's been diagnosed with lung cancer."

She nodded. "It's terminal."

"Until we get some of the test results back, we're going to make Herbert as comfortable as possible and make sure he gets plenty of rest and fluids. Keeping him on a higher output of oxygen is key right now to getting his heart rate and other levels back to where they should be."

When they'd planned this trip, they hadn't planned for Pops having a hospital stay. They were supposed to leave in a couple of days. What were they going to do now?

How long would they be here? "Will you be admitting him then?"

"Not until we can determine what is going on. Once I have answers, I'll be sure to inform you of the next steps." He looked at her. "From what I understand, there isn't much that can be done for your grandfather. Have you discussed palliative care for him?"

She paled and felt her legs grow weak. "Hospice, you mean?" Oh man. Were they really at that point already?

GUS FELT SOMEONE put a hand on his arm. He shook himself awake to find Cec standing beside him. "Why don't you go back to the cabin and get some real sleep? We're still waiting on test results, and it could be hours before we know anything."

Her eyes were weary and a little bit sad. She looked exhausted. "What about you?" he asked. "What are you planning on doing?"

"I need to stay here with him."

"Then I'll stay too."

She glanced around the waiting room. "What happened to Phyllis?"

"I convinced her to go home and get

some rest, and I promised that we'd call with any updates."

"Of course." She looked at him. "You should go, really. I'll be fine on my own here."

"You forget that the emergency room is practically my former home. Doesn't matter if it's up north or back in Detroit. It's what I know. What I'm familiar with."

"Still, that doesn't mean you have to stay."

"I'm staying for you, Cec." He wanted to reach out and pull her down to him. To hold her until her fears and worries melted away. But that wasn't the kind of relationship they had. After all, they'd decided by the waterfall to let whatever was going on between them fall away. But that didn't mean he couldn't be a friend to her, so he reached out and took her hand and gave it a squeeze. "Did you call your mom?"

She shook her head. "I figured I'd wait until we had some answers. Why have her worry until we know if there's something to be concerned about?"

"Good point." He hadn't spent much time with Anna, but he did know that Burt meant as much to her as he did to Cec. "Go back and stay with Burt. I'll be waiting for you out here when you get any news, good or bad, okay?"

She blinked a few times, looking at him until she gave a soft nod and squeezed his hand once before letting go and walking back to Burt's room.

Gus settled in and took out his phone. Since this was a holiday weekend, answers would probably take longer to come than they'd want. Might as well keep himself busy playing a game or two.

CEC STIRRED WHEN she heard the door to the room open, and a nurse stepped inside to check on Pops's vitals. "Sorry, miss. I didn't mean to wake you."

"It's okay. I wasn't really asleep."

The nurse checked the heart monitor and made notes on her tablet. Cec didn't know what any of the numbers on the machine meant except for the one that showed her grandfather's oxygen levels hadn't risen above eighty percent since she'd arrived. Not good. He needed to have those levels in the nineties, and she hadn't seen them this low in a while.

"Any test results back yet from the lab?"

"Some." The nurse gave her a smile. "It's probably going to be a long night until we get all of them."

"His oxygen levels aren't improving."

"That could take a while. The machines he's on now are giving him more oxygen than the tanks were, so the levels will get better over time."

"But he's not bouncing back as fast as he should, is he?"

Cec got to her feet and walked to the bed where Pops rested. He'd been mostly sleeping since she'd arrived, which was probably a good thing considering that his body needed the rest. She brushed the bangs away from his forehead, and he stirred a little but didn't wake up. "He seems to be sleeping pretty well, at least."

The nurse nodded then asked, "Is there anything I can get you while we wait?"

Cec shook her head and took her perch in the chair beside Pops's bed.

She dozed off again and woke when the door opened hours later. The emergency room doctor entered. "Ma'am, can we talk out in the hallway?"

That didn't sound good. She rose to her feet and shuffled out the door, following the doctor. "Miss Karsten, are you here at the hospital alone?"

"No, our friend Gus is in the waiting room. Why? What's going on?"

The doctor took a deep breath before saying, "There's fluid building up in Herbert's lungs that is causing the shortness of breath and chest pain."

"Like pneumonia?"

"Not quite. The cause for his is the cancer growing at a faster rate than before."

Cec took a step back and hit the wall behind her. "He's getting worse?" She put a hand to her eyes and tried to keep calm. "So how do we fix this?"

"Herbert informed us he doesn't want us to do anything beyond basic care. We can give him morphine and increase the output of oxygen, but this is only going to keep him comfortable."

She had the medical directive for Pops in her purse, so she knew the doctor was telling the truth. She didn't want to ask but had to. "Is he going to die?"

"Not tonight."

"But soon?"

"Each patient is different, but given his age and health, it could be a month, maybe."

She stared at the doctor. "A month." She nodded and glanced at the closed door. "Do I tell him?"

"According to Herbert, he's aware of the possibility. And he's accepted it."

Well, she hadn't. She needed more than thirty days. She needed thirty years, and it still wouldn't be enough. "Thank you, doctor. I need to let Gus know."

"I'm sorry, Miss Karsten. I wish I had better news."

She walked to the waiting room and found Gus staring at a television that showed an infomercial. He turned his head to look at her when she called his name. And in a moment, he was out of the chair and holding her to him. Her tears dampened his T-shirt as she shared what the doctor had said. He rubbed her back and held her, and she clung to him, grateful for the contact.

When she finished talking, he led her to a chair and sat down next to her. "So, what do we do now? Are they going to admit him?"

"They're making him comfortable, but there's not much they can do beyond giving him oxygen and morphine because of his medical directive. They haven't said anything about admitting him, and I don't think Pops would agree to it anyways."

"Then we should see what he wants to do. Does he want to stay here or go back to the cabin? Or should we take a chance and make the trip back home?"

The possibilities made her head swim, and a wave of fatigue threatened to take her down. "I don't know."

Gus pressed a kiss to the top of her head. "This is tough, but you're a strong woman, Cecily. It's going to be okay."

"I wish we hadn't come here."

"Our trip had nothing to do with this."

"But what if it did?"

"You saw him at his old house this morning when he found the hiding spot and then the carving on the tree. You've seen him when Phyllis is around. That's good medicine for him. A lot more positive than sitting in the house in Thora and waiting to die."

"I'm glad you're here. I don't think I could do this on my own."

"I'm glad I could be here for you."

She looked into his eyes, his sincerity clear. She glanced behind her. "I should get back to Pops. Do you think you could call Phyllis with the update?"

"Of course."

"And I'll call my mom after I check on Pops." She started to walk away, then turned to find Gus watching her. "Thank you again."

CEC RETURNED FROM the cafeteria with a cup of coffee and put her hand on the door to her grandfather's room just as the door opened, and Phyllis rushed out. The older woman brushed past her and down the hall. Cec stared after her and called, "Phyllis? What's wrong? Is it Pops? Is he…"

"He's fine." Phyllis turned to her and shook her head. "But I shouldn't be here."

Cec took a few steps toward her. "Of course you should. I haven't seen my grandfather as happy as he is when he's with you. He hasn't been this positive in a very long time. You're good for him."

Phyllis dropped her gaze to the floor. "I thought I might be too, but..." She looked up at Cec. "We were fooling ourselves these last few days. We even talked about the possibility of him staying here longer. But with how things are right now, Burt and I have come to accept that our story needs to end now."

That couldn't be right. Not with the way that she'd seen them look at each other. There had to be something else, even if it was only for the next month. "I know it looks pretty bad at the moment, but he has bounced back before. He could do it again."

Phyllis's half smile was weak. "I hope that he does, but... We decided it was best for us to say our goodbyes. I'm sorry, so very sorry."

Phyllis hurried away, and Cec stared after her. Cec then stood at the closed door and summoned a little courage. She entered the hospital room to find Pops staring out the window, his arms crossed over his chest. He turned to her as she approached the bed.

"Where's Gus?" he asked.

"He's making a few phone calls, checking on the status of his car." She tried to look in his eyes to see if she could figure out what was going on with him. "What happened with Phyllis?"

"We said goodbye." He gave a shrug as if he didn't care, but Cec could see that he did.

Cec checked the monitors, but the numbers hadn't changed much. He'd been in the hospital less than twelve hours, but progress was slow. His oxygen level still hadn't reached ninety percent. She noticed one of his legs was exposed, so she adjusted the blanket.

"Would you please stop fussing with those blankets? They're fine the way they are." Pops scowled at Cec, and she dropped the covers and stepped away from the bed.

Gus smiled, standing in the open doorway. He chuckled as he entered the room. "You're back to being crotchety, so you must be feeling better."

Pops seemed agitated. "I just want to get out of here. You think you can do something about that?"

Gus's eyebrows lifted at his tone. "Maybe we should call Phyllis and ask her to come back for a visit. Maybe that will put you in a better mood."

Pops looked down at the blankets. "There's no need to call her."

Cec risked Pops's wrath and pressed for an explanation. "Why did you tell her goodbye? Or is it that you asked her to leave?"

Gus looked completely confused, his head bobbing as he glanced from Pops to her and back again to her grandfather. "Why would you ask her to leave? I thought things were going well between you two."

Pops mumbled something, and Cec stepped closer to the bed. "Do you want to stay here a little longer than we planned?"

"No."

"Do you want to go back home?"

Pops said, scowling, "What I want isn't what I'm going to get, so we might as well go home and let me die there. And the sooner, the better."

Cec was still bewildered and exchanged a brief questioning glance with Gus. What was going on with her grandfather? "What happened when Phyllis was here earlier?" she asked him.

Pops huffed. "Can't a man want to go home without it being a big deal?"

Cec gently put a hand on top of his. "Pops, what changed? You two were having a great time together."

"I refuse to let her watch me die." He glared at them both. "Happy now? She already played nurse and buried one husband. It's not fair of me to ask her to do that again. So that's that. Why not just say goodbye while we still have a chance?"

"Oh, Pops. Did you even ask her what she wanted?"

"It doesn't matter anymore what either one of us wants. Having those chest pains last night only reminded me that I'm on borrowed time."

Cec leaned over to give him a hug, but the man tried to wriggle away from her. "Get off. I'm fine."

Cec refused to let go of him and laid her head on his shoulder. "I'm so sorry, Pops. I know how much you wanted this."

He gave a half-hearted shrug before lay-ing his head back on the pillow and closing his eyes.

Cec stood and turned to Gus. "What did you find out from the mechanic? Could we make arrangements and leave now?"

"I was finally able to get through to him. I explained the situation and how we need to get my SUV back right away. He's going to put a rush on it, so it will be ready later this evening."

She nodded and glanced at Pops, who was now turned on his side, his back toward them. She pointed to the door. "Can we go talk in the hallway for a minute?"

Gus followed her from the room. She spoke in a low voice. "I think we should pack up our things at the cabin. Pops seems pretty intent on going home, and I think we should do what we can to give him what he wants."

Gus was staring at Burt's door. "I don't know about you, but I didn't see it ending like that. I thought the two of them really had something."

"I guess when you know there's not going to be a happy ending, it's harder to take a risk and put your heart on the line."

"Is that how Burt feels? Or you?" When she started to protest, he quickly apologized. "I'm sorry, I didn't mean that. Forget it." He gazed at his feet for a moment before looking up at her. "I tell you what. If you want, I can go and get our things from the cabin while you stay here with Burt. Talk to the doctor. Let's get him discharged and we can drive home as soon as my car is ready."

She nodded and thanked him. "I don't want to be gone too long from him. The doctor says he's out of the woods for now, but it could change at any time."

Gus put a hand on her arm. "I understand."

She held his gaze. "This trip didn't go at all like we planned."

"It started off pretty well, but you're right. I hadn't envisioned this ending for any of us."

CEC DOZED IN the chair beside the hospital bed and startled when Pops called her name. She jumped up. "Are you okay? What's wrong?"

"Nothing's wrong." Pops shifted his body

around. "Can't get comfortable. When are they going to let me out of here?"

"They want to make sure you're stable before they release you."

"I want to get out of here."

"I know. I'm working on it."

He frowned. "Then work harder. I don't care what you have to do, but I need to leave. Now."

"Pops…"

"There's nothing more they can do for me. I don't care if I have to sign something that says I was released against medical advice, but you need to get me out of here."

Cec put a hand on his arm. "Let your breathing get back to normal."

"There is no normal anymore. Don't you get that?"

Cec took a step back. This angry man was not someone she recognized. Pops usually kept his cool. And he never snapped at her.

Pops winced, his expression sheepish. "I'm sorry, baby girl. I shouldn't have yelled like that."

"Why do you want to leave so soon?"

"I did what I came to do, so now it's time to go home. There's nothing they can do for me now, so why should we wait around? I can die at home as easily as I can here."

"You're not going to die."

"Not today, but it won't be long." He took a deep breath and stared off into the distance. "I'm ready to go."

"Because things didn't work out with Phyllis?"

"Not just because of her. I've done everything I wanted to do."

She peered at him, not believing a word of that. "You've done everything you wanted on this trip?"

Pops shrugged. "Okay, not everything but enough that I don't have any regrets."

Cec sat on the edge of his bed. "What didn't you get to do?"

Pops took her hand in his. "I didn't get to see things through with you and Gus."

"What things did you think would happen between me and Gus?"

He gave a shrug. "Gus already knows that you're a terrific woman who has a lot to offer him. And I'd hoped to convince you that he could be a good man for you."

"That's why you kept pushing the two

of us together on this trip and spending so much time alone?"

"Maybe." Pops colored slightly, then cleared his throat. "Okay, I definitely did. But I guess it didn't work."

"What makes you say that?"

Pops peered at her, and it was her turn for her cheeks to get warm. "Did something happen when I wasn't looking?"

She glanced away from him rather than looking into his eyes that shone with hope. "It doesn't matter. We're returning soon to our normal lives, and there isn't a future for us. He'll be moving here in a few weeks for his new job."

Pops made a noise and settled further into the blankets. "I'll be dying soon, and I want to make sure you are taken care of."

"I'll be fine. You don't have to worry about me."

"You know, I had a good life. These last few days showed me that I was blessed with a wonderful family and marriage. And while I might have hoped that I could have a little longer with Phyllis, I can't complain."

A while passed before Cec added, "And

now you have some closure on that part of your life."

"Closure." Pops made a noise at the back of his throat. "You young people are so concerned about having everything tied up in a neat little package, but let me tell you something that I've learned in my eight decades of life. Nothing about this life is tidy or neat. It's messy. And chaotic. And more often than not, it doesn't make sense no matter how hard you try to understand it."

He paused. "But in the end, even the messy bits of your life are overshadowed by the beautiful parts. And those are the things I'll take with me."

THEY HAD BEEN on the road to Thora for almost four hours, driving straight through as much as they could. Burt had signed himself out of the hospital against medical advice, but with him now being placed under hospice care, the doctor was limited as to what he could do. Burt had fallen asleep in the back seat within a few minutes of leaving the parking lot of the hospital.

Gus glanced at Cec, who sat in the passenger seat, staring out the window. She hadn't said much since they'd left, but then neither had Gus. He cleared his throat, then leaned over to turn the volume down on the radio. "I could use a break. How about you?"

She turned to look at him. "I can take over driving when we stop."

Gus gave a nod. "I'd appreciate that since we're getting home as soon as we can. No detours this time." He took a deep breath and stretched in his seat.

"I figure we can probably make it by tomorrow morning if we drive straight through."

"My mom said she'll meet us at the house so she can help us with him. I'll have to call her when we get closer to home."

They fell silent, the hum of the tires on the road spreading a lull inside the car. A sign for a gas station appeared on the horizon, alerting them they could take a break in the next mile. Shortly after seeing the sign, Gus pulled into the station. "I'll get some gas while we're here. We still have a half tank left, but this way we can keep going."

Cec put her hand on the door handle. "While you do that, I'll get some snacks."

Gus checked on Burt, who stirred in his sleep but was otherwise fine. He stepped out of the car and began pumping gas. Cec returned with a bag full of snacks and drinks. "I wasn't sure what you wanted, so I bought a variety. They did have a bag of your favorite chips."

"Perfect."

She began to get back inside the car when Gus added, "Before we get home, I think we should talk about what happened between us, don't you?"

"I didn't realize there was anything else to talk about," she said.

"How about what I told you the other day at the waterfall?"

"As I recall, you said you didn't want to fall for me. And that we need to step back from spending so much time together."

Had he really said that? It seemed like he had, but he'd been wrong. "That's true, but I've been thinking—"

"I've been thinking too. And you were right. We're completely wrong for each other. You're reckless. I'm cautious. You want to travel the world, while I'm content being at home in Thora. I like following the rules while you like to break them." She paused to take a breath, as if to collect her thoughts. "I've really enjoyed this time getting to know you better, but we're heading back to the real world. And that means we have separate lives. And separate futures."

He took a step toward her. "What if I was wrong about all that?"

"But that's the thing. You weren't, and I finally see that now." She patted his chest. "I'm glad we became good friends."

"Friends."

She nodded and smiled, then held her hand out toward him. "I'll take the next part of the driving. Maybe you can get some rest."

He pulled the keys out of his shorts pocket and handed them to her. "Cec…"

She closed her hand over the keys and gave his hand a light squeeze before walking to the driver's side and slipping into the car.

He turned back to look at the pump. It had finished filling the tank while he'd been trying to reveal his heart to Cecily.

To tell her that seeing Burt fighting for his last days reminded him of what was truly important. Not jobs or seeing the world. Not chasing the next thrill. It was the relationships, the people, that counted.

But instead of handing her his future, she'd handed back his heart.

CEC UNPACKED THE SUV while her mom and Gus helped Pops settle into his bed. Hauling out suitcases and backpacks helped her keep her mind on what would happen next. She'd have to make a list of things to do. Call the doctor and the hospice nurse to notify them that they had returned. Try to get a delivery of new oxygen tanks. Maybe see if she could get higher airflow tubing that would increase the oxygen output from the condenser.

"Hey."

Cec placed the last suitcase on the floor in the kitchen and looked up to find Gus watching her. "Burt's resting, but he asked if you would stop by his room and talk to him before he goes back to sleep."

"Everything okay?"

Gus nodded, then picked up his duffel

bag. "I left my medical bag in his room for now, in case you need any supplies. You'll probably have to get a delivery soon."

"Already on my to-do list." She handed him his backpack. "Thank you. For everything."

He took the bag from her, but she kept her hand on the strap. "Of course. My pleasure." He looked at her, and she couldn't stop looking at him. Finally, he said, "I should get home. It's late."

"Or early, since the sun should be up in about an hour." She let go of the strap. "Thanks again."

He reached over and gave her a quick, awkward hug. She felt him press a soft kiss to her cheek. "Goodbye."

Then he walked out of the kitchen, through the garage and back to his house.

Cec swallowed and reached up to feel the warm spot on her cheek where he had kissed her.

"Cecily? Pops is asking for you."

She turned to find her mother looking at her. "Gus told me."

Her mom frowned. "Are you okay, sweetie? You look like you could use a good cry."

"It's been a long week. I'll tell you more about it after I go see Pops." She rubbed her mom's arm as she walked past her.

When she entered the bedroom, Pops looked asleep, so she backed up and was about to close the door when she heard him call her name. She stepped back inside. "Pops, you should be sleeping now. We can talk tomorrow. Whatever it is, it can wait."

He patted the bed beside him. "We'll talk now."

She hesitated, then went to the bed and took a seat next to him. Pops placed her hands in his and looked up at her. "I…"

He started to cough, and Cec rose to her feet searching for…she didn't know what exactly but something to help him. He waved her to sit back down. "I'm fine. It's just a cough."

This time, she didn't sit but stood beside him. "I'll call the doctor in the morning. Maybe we can get an appointment for you later this week."

Pops shook his head. "No more appointments. Please. I'm sick and tired of doctors."

"You should be checked out. After what happened up north…"

"I'm as good as I'm going to get. So, it's time to let that go." He took her hand in his again. "What happened between you and Gus?"

Cec laughed at his words. "That's what you want to talk to me about?" Her shoulders dropped an inch. "Then you might as well go to sleep because there's nothing to discuss. I told you before, there is no me and Gus."

"Why not? I thought you two were developing a connection."

"We're friends, Pops, but I'm afraid we'll have to disappoint your romantic aspirations for us. Besides, Gus will probably take that job up in Lighthouse Bay. He's going to be leaving."

"So, give him a reason to stay."

She leaned forward and kissed his forehead. "Get some rest. It's the best thing for you right now."

"I slept most of the way home. I'm not tired."

"Still. You should try to sleep." She could feel tears threatening. "I'm sorry the trip wasn't everything you wanted it to be."

"I got answers. And I got to say my good-byes. That's what is most important."

She adjusted the bed covers and brought them up to his chin. "So did I." Switching off the light, she went to leave. "Good night, Pops."

"Good night, baby girl."

She stepped out into the hall and closed the door, then leaned her head against it.

CHAPTER FOURTEEN

A COUPLE DAYS passed since they'd arrived home, and Gus hadn't seen Cec. He'd caught glimpses of her when he walked next door to visit Pops, but she seemed to always have a reason to be somewhere he wasn't when he was next door.

"You could go out of your way to find her, you know."

Gus turned back to Pops, who sat in his recliner, a bottle of beer in one hand, a baseball game on the television. "Who?"

Pops gave him a look. "The woman you're always looking for when you're here with me."

"Cecily?" Gus shook his head. "I'm just looking around to make sure you've got everything you need. How are you feeling?"

"The same as I was when you asked me twenty minutes ago." Pops peered at him. "What happened between you two?"

"Nothing. Why? What did she say?"

"Same."

The crack of a bat on the television screen caught their attention, and silence fell between them again. During a commercial, Gus said, "I'll be heading back up north early tomorrow morning."

"You're taking that job?"

"Still considering it. But I thought I'd go visit my friend Alex for a few days. Check out his resort a little more and see if it would be a good fit for me."

Pops nodded. "Sounds like a good plan."

"On one hand, it's a great offer that will give me some of what I've been looking for. And on the other hand..." Gus sighed and took a sip of his beer, letting that thought drop.

"On the other hand, there's Cecily."

Gus glanced at Pops, then back to the television screen. "She's not a factor in my decision. She's made that very clear."

"Really? I guess I was as wrong about you two as I was about Phyllis and me."

The ball game came back on, but Gus only half watched it. Instead, he wondered about Burt's words. Cec wasn't a factor in decisions about his future, but his confusion about her was clouding his ability to make a choice about what to do. Cec was special to him, but was it enough? Was she even open to it?

"Do you regret looking for Phyllis again? Knowing what you do now, would you still go find her?"

Burt stayed silent for a moment, then spoke. "Things might not have ended the way I wanted them to, but those few days I had with her again…" He gave a soft smile. "I wouldn't trade those for anything."

A prick of jealousy hit Gus in the chest at that smile. He rose to his feet. "Well, I should get going. Long trip tomorrow." He walked to the recliner and patted Burt on the back before leaning down to give him a hug.

"She's down in the basement."

Gus straightened. "I wasn't asking."

"I thought you might want to go say goodbye at least."

Gus looked at the older man, whose eyes twinkled at him before turning his attention back to the baseball game.

CEC WROTE ON the box with a black marker to indicate it was to be donated, then stacked it on the other boxes with the same destination. She turned and put her hands on her hips to survey the progress she'd made. When she'd decided to start organizing the basement, she hadn't expected to find so much stuff down here.

"There's a lot of history in this basement."

She turned her head to find Gus standing at the base of the stairs. "Which is why I've been working on going through it, slowly and carefully."

He leaned down and put a hand on an old, red tricycle. "This has got to be what? Fifty years old?"

"Closer to sixty. It was my dad's when he was little."

"They really made things to last back then." He straightened and looked at her. "Have you been avoiding me?"

Her head jerked back at the direct question. "No. Just giving you the space you wanted. That we agreed upon."

"Right, we did." He gave a nod, then walked farther into the basement. "I'll be leaving for the UP tomorrow. Would you mind picking up my mail and watching my house while I'm gone?"

"Sure. How long are you planning on going?"

"Don't know for certain yet. A few days at least." He looked at her. "It depends."

"On what?"

"How things go there. Plus, there's Burt. And you."

"Me? What do I have to do with the length of your trip up north?"

He crossed the basement to stand in front of her, staring at her with an odd expression. "I'm not sure how else to ask this, so I'll just ask, have you missed me these last couple of days?"

She held his gaze but didn't answer. She had missed him, and she wondered if he had missed her. She couldn't stop thinking of him. Wanting to see him, talk to him. She'd avoided him because she was afraid he might see that she wanted to be with him. A lot. Maybe too much.

"Because I've missed you like crazy."

Well, that answered that question. "Gus…"

"I've wondered what you would do if I walked up to you like this and put my hands here." He settled them on her hips and nudged her closer to him. "And what if I leaned in toward you..."

She tipped her head back, and he pressed his mouth to hers. She gave a long sigh against his lips as he deepened the kiss and pulled her fully into his arms. She relished the feel of him against her body, but she couldn't help thinking that this was wrong. Their timing was all wrong. He was leaving.

She pressed her hand against his chest and he backed away. "Gus...we agreed."

"And I think it was the worst thing I ever agreed to. I don't know what I was thinking, actually. I'm not even sure if I can be friends with you, given how strongly I feel about you. That sounds ridiculous now that I've said it out loud." He kept staring at her and she refused to look away. "I want more than being buddies. Or neighbors. Don't you?"

"Regardless of what I might want, I can't give you more than that if you can't offer me more than just tomorrow. I want forever, I've realized. What my grandparents had. Because you were right about me. I'm not interested in a temporary fling."

"I know but…"

Resolved, she crossed her arms over her chest and took a step back. "Are you turning down the job at Alex's resort?"

He pursed his lips and looked down at the floor. "I don't know. I haven't decided. But I'll be here until Burt…"

She winced at the words he didn't say, her heart well and truly broken. "Then there's nothing else to discuss. Have a safe trip."

She went over to the other side of the basement and switched on another lamp, chasing away the last of the shadows. A box of ancient clothes was waiting for her to sort through it, so she got to work. She waited until she heard his steps on the stairs before turning to where he had been standing, wishing with all her might that things could be different.

HIS CAST LANDED perfectly in the lake, and Gus wound the reel to tighten the line before leaning against the edge of the boat. When Alex had woken him up early that morning with the suggestion to go fishing, he'd jumped at the chance and had been dressed and ready within five minutes. Now, as he lounged in the stern of Alex's boat, he was appreciating the spontaneous moment, but at the same time, conflicted.

This seemed like his answer to the job question. He could live every day like this, time pretty much his own, if he accepted the opportunity that Alex dangled in front of him. Tempting, so why the hesitation? Why couldn't he give Alex a yes answer?

"You look deep in thought. What's going on?"

Gus glanced over at Alex, who relaxed at the bow of the boat. "Just thinking about how good the last couple of days have been. Thanks again for the invitation."

"Does that mean you've decided about my job offer?"

Gus gave a shrug, then jerked as the bobber on his line dipped into the water. He bent forward and started to wind the reel to bring back the line. But he pulled too quickly, and the easy slack told him that the fish had gotten away.

"You almost had that one."

"Story of my life, man."

"So what is stopping you from accepting the job? Is it the salary? Because we can negotiate that. Or the location? I know we're fairly remote out here, but you won't find natural beauty like this elsewhere."

"It's none of those things."

"But there is something that's keeping you from taking it. So, explain it to me. Maybe we can find a way around it."

"Part of it is Burt. He doesn't have much time left, and I want to be there to help out his family."

Alex nodded. "I'd like to have you on staff by the end of this month, but it's flexible. I can wait. But something tells me your indecision has to do with Cecily too."

Gus hesitated. "No, we're just friends." Though he'd hoped for something more. "There's nothing going on there."

"You can fool yourself by saying that, but Rose and I have eyes. We saw how the two of you were looking at each other, and there was a lot more than friendship in those glances." Alex pulled in his line and rebaited the empty hook. "Listen. When I met Rosie, I was saving up money to move to New York and open a restaurant with my brother. But one look at her, and all my plans went out the window. And I haven't regretted it for a moment. Never looked back since."

"You don't understand. I'm no good at relationships."

"Says who?"

"Two failed marriages, that's who." He pulled in his line and rebaited it. That fish had enjoyed all the food but had avoided the hook. "Looks like the fish are biting, but they're not getting hooked."

"Is that your life plan as well? To enjoy the bait without getting hooked? To spend the rest of your life in pursuit of short-term relationships that don't go anywhere? And you're happy with that?"

He thought about the last short-term relationship he'd had. It had lasted a couple of weeks and when it had started to become serious, he'd broken it off with no one's feelings hurt. His heart was intact. He'd liked her but hadn't given himself the chance to fall for her. Or anyone. The emotions just weren't there.

And then there was Cecily, who he could fall for so easily. If he hadn't already. But she was a forever kind of person, just like they both said, and he clearly wasn't.

CEC STOOD IN the darkened kitchen and stared out the window at the house next door. Gus had only been gone three days but it had felt like a lifetime. The thump of Pops's walker alerted her to his presence.

Watching her from the doorway, he said, "I was in the mood for a snack."

She went and flipped on the overhead light and walked to the cupboard. "We've got crackers. Pretzels. Or if you want something sweet, I've got cookies." She turned to look at him. "Or I bought some of that fruit salad you liked. I can get you a bowl of that."

He seemed to wait for her to offer something else. "The fruit, I guess."

He took a seat at the table while she got the plastic container of fruit salad from the refrigerator. When she'd put a couple of spoonfuls in a bowl, she brought that along with a fork to the table and claimed a seat next to him.

"Thanks." He stabbed a blueberry, then

looked at her. "You could call him, you know."

She tightened her lips and shook her head. He didn't need to say who he was referring to. She knew. "I don't have anything to say to him."

"How about you don't want him to take that job? That you want him to stay here? That's a pretty good start."

"What does it matter to me if he takes that job or not?"

Pops shrugged as he chewed the blueberry. "I don't know. I thought he might have become important to you during the road trip. Guess I was wrong."

She smoothed the lace doily that her grandmother had crocheted long ago. She'd found it in one of the boxes in the basement and had brought it up to decorate the center of the kitchen table. "What Gus does is up to him. I have no say in the matter."

"What if you did have a say?"

She frowned. "Pops, the man never stays longer than a couple of years in one place. What kind of future do you think he'd offer me? He's already looking to leave."

"Because he's been drifting through life

without an anchor and looking for a place to call home. So be that for him."

"I can't."

"Why not?"

"Because I can't be the reason he stays."

Pops rolled his eyes at this. "Youth is wasted on the young."

"Look at you. You wanted Phyllis to be the reason you stayed up north, and you couldn't do it. So why should I for Gus?"

"That was a different situation. Gus isn't dying."

"The way he jumps off waterfalls, it's only a matter of time."

Pops reached over and took her hand in his. "Baby girl, it's only a matter of time for all of us."

She fell silent, and Pops let go of her hand and returned to eating his fruit. Once he finished, he set the fork in the empty bowl. "There's something else I want to talk to you about. I have an idea, and I know you're going to hate it."

"Another road trip?" She didn't think she could handle it.

"No. A party."

She stared at him. "You want to have a party?"

"I got to thinking. At someone's funeral, all these people say nice things about the person who died. And they get no thanks, no response. So, I want to do all that and hold the funeral before I die."

"I thought you didn't want a funeral."

"A going-away party then. We'll invite a bunch of family and friends. They can make speeches or toasts or whatever. And I can say goodbye to them one last time." He looked at her, hopeful. "I've already started a guest list of who I want to invite."

"Pops, this is…" But she could see how much this meant to him, so she changed tack. "This is one of the better ideas you've had. Fine. Let's see who is on this list."

GUS STEPPED AWAY from the trail to answer his ringing phone. "Hey, Burt. How are you feeling?"

"Not bad for a crotchety old man. Where are you right now?"

"Out on a hiking trail and admiring the trees." He chuckled. "You were right about Lighthouse Bay. It's beautiful."

"So, you've made up your mind then."

"Not quite. But it's going to be hard to turn down this opportunity."

Burt sighed on the other end. "Listen. Do you think you'll be free on Saturday? I'm throwing a party."

The older man told him the details about his last goodbye. Gus was excited. "I'll be sure to be free then."

"Good. Good."

"How's Cecily doing?"

"Why don't you call her and ask her yourself?"

LATER THE NEXT DAY, Gus made his way home and found to his surprise a strange car parked in his driveway. It had been a long journey so all he wanted to do was fall onto his bed and sleep until maybe the weekend. Instead, intrigued, he approached the car, but no one was in it. Very odd. He paused when he heard voices coming from the backyard next door. He walked around the side of the house to find Cec and Burt sitting in lawn chairs in their backyard with someone he instantly recognized. "Mom, what are you doing here?"

He rushed forward to embrace her as she stood up from her seat. She hugged him back then put a hand on his cheek. "I missed this face."

He gave her another embrace. "How did you know I would be back today?"

"I didn't, but I hoped that you would. Burt and Cec here offered to let me stay with them if you didn't make it back in time."

Cec gave him a quick nod when he turned to her. She looked as good as he remembered, but her eyes darted away when he tried to hold her gaze. "Well, thank you both."

Burt held up a glass of iced tea. "Why don't you sit down and join us? I was just inviting your mom to come to my party this weekend."

Gus glanced at her. "Will you be here? How long were you planning on staying?"

She smiled at him. "I'll be here." She turned to Burt. "And I'd love to come to your party. It sounds like it's going to be a good time."

"I plan on that." Burt started to cough and covered his mouth. Cec handed him a tissue, then put her hand on his shoulder until the coughing subsided. "My apologies, folks. Seems like I'm doing that more and more lately."

Cec rose to her feet. "Maybe we should get you back inside, Pops. Matt just cut the lawn for us today so maybe that's irritating your lungs."

She paused in front of him first. "Glad you made it home okay."

Before he could reply, she turned back to Burt and helped him into the house. Gus led his mom back to her car where she retrieved her suitcase from the trunk of the rental car. "You were right about Burt. He's a good man."

"He's my best friend."

"And you're right about his granddaughter, too."

Shocked, he glanced around, hoping that no one was within listening distance. Still, he lowered his voice. "Mom, I never told you about Cecily," he whispered.

"Maybe you should have." She gave him a look. "Now are you going to invite me in or not?"

He headed up to the porch and unlocked the front door before taking her suitcase from her hand. "I'll show you where you'll be sleeping."

Once he reached the guest bedroom, he laid the suitcase on the bed and turned to find his mom staring at him. "Why do I feel like I'm about to get a lecture?"

"Do you think you need one?" She took a seat on the bed then patted the empty spot next to her. "From the looks of you, you've been doing a pretty good job beating up on yourself."

"I wouldn't say beating up, exactly."

"Then what would you call it?"

He recalled the thoughts he'd been turning over in his mind the last few weeks. "I failed twice at making a marriage work. So why am I even considering a relationship with Cecily? It's doomed before it's even started."

His mom gave a low whistle. "That's a pretty harsh view of yourself."

"Face it, mom. I'm a big loser when it comes to relationships. I can't make it last."

"I get it. I felt the same way when things went sour between me and your dad. I figured that I would spend the rest of my life alone because if I couldn't make it work with him, then I couldn't make it work with anyone else. Then I met Roy."

"And you somehow knew that it would be a happily ever after?"

His mom laughed, shaking her head. "Goodness, no. When things got serious, I broke up with him because I thought that I couldn't make him happy. Couldn't make it work."

"What did he do to convince you otherwise?"

"Nothing. He gave me the space and the time to figure it out on my own." She took one of Gus's hands in hers. "Son, just because your marriages failed in the past doesn't make you a failure. And it doesn't doom every future relationship to fail either. You deserve to find your happiness."

"I don't know, mom."

"I do. Roy and I are as happy as we've ever been."

Gus squeezed his mom's hand. "You've given me something to think about."

"Great." She patted his leg with her free hand. "Now get out of here and let me have a little rest. You look like you could use some yourself."

He leaned forward and kissed her cheek. "Good night, mom. Love you."

She smiled then gave him a hug. "I love you, too. And think about what I said."

As he lay in bed that night, he played the conversation over and over in his mind. What if he was wrong and he could be a forever kind of man?

THE FRONT DOOR swung open unexpectedly, and BJ ran into the living room, arms opened wide. "Here I am!"

Pops got to his feet, showing energy that he hadn't had in days. "BJ!" He put his arms around him and held on tight. "Why didn't anyone tell me you were coming home?"

Pops turned to Cec who had followed her brother into the house. "Wouldn't be a surprise if I had told you, would it?"

He waggled his finger at her, but gave a wide smile before hugging BJ again. "You'll be here for my party tomorrow then. I thought you said…"

"I wouldn't miss it, Pops. You know that."

Pops was smiling, then started to cough. Cec rushed forward, handing him a handkerchief that seemed to always be near these days. He accepted it and pressed it to his mouth. After a few moments, he cleared his throat. "Sorry about that."

BJ swallowed, looking pale. "It's okay. You don't have to apologize."

Their mom appeared from the direction of the kitchen and went to put an arm around Pops's shoulders. "Why don't we all sit down so you and BJ can catch up?"

Her mom led Pops to his recliner and helped him get situated, and BJ took the seat closest to Pops. "I'm sorry I haven't gotten here sooner."

Pops waved off the comment. "Don't be silly. You've got your comedy career about to take off. So tell me, how did your last gig go?"

BJ started telling him about it while Cec glanced at her mom. "Thank you for staying with Pops while I went to meet BJ at the airport."

"Of course." She gestured toward BJ. "He's looking thinner than he did back at Christmas, don't you think?"

"I think we all are. Stress and worry will do that."

"I don't know. After your dad died, I'm pretty sure that I ate my way through my grief. But you haven't done that with Tom."

"Tom didn't die."

"No, but your marriage ended." Anna looked her over. "But your grief has more to do with Pops."

"He's getting worse. He's more tired than usual. But then that's not a surprise given all that's happened." She pointed at her mom. "And you're still planning on moving in to help me?"

Her mom nodded. "After his fall last week, I think I should. He's going to get to a point where you can't take care of him on your own. And that's what I'm here for. To help you."

"Thank you. Gus promised he would help me too, but I'm not sure what his plans are now. If he takes that job up north..."

This time her mom put an arm around her shoulder and leaned into her. "I'm guessing you haven't told him your feelings then."

"There's nothing to tell."

"Right." Anna let out a big sigh then said louder to be heard by them all, "I don't know about anyone else, but I don't feel like cooking dinner. Which neighbor's casserole should we gratefully try tonight?"

PEOPLE FILLED THE kitchen and spilled out into the backyard where Pops sat in a lawn chair like a king on his throne, watching over the festivities. Cec smiled at her mother before pouring another plastic cup with lemonade. She checked the food, then turned to find her best friend, Vivi, standing there with her boyfriend Brian.

Vivi smiled and said, "Everything looks great."

"Thanks. Pops and I have been going over the details for this party for over a week. And he had definite ideas about what he wanted." She gave a grin. "And didn't want."

Vivi glanced around the kitchen. "Is the mysterious Gus here yet? I'd love to finally meet him."

"He returned from his trip up north a couple days ago, but I haven't really seen him much. His mom is in town so he's been busy with her. But I'm sure he'll be by eventually. I know he wouldn't want to miss Pops's party."

Brian put his arm around Vivi. "Speaking of, I think we should go pay our regards to the guest of honor."

Cec's mom walked up and got a cup of iced tea. "You did a great job, kiddo. I can't believe so many people came on such short notice. It's so considerate, I know Pops is loving this."

"We're all set for our other surprise visitor, right? You haven't seen her yet?"

"No. She said she'd call when she gets close to the house." Anna took in the crowd of people laughing and mingling. "By the way, have you seen your brother? I thought I heard his voice earlier, but when I turned it wasn't him."

"Last I saw him he was setting up the music system in the backyard."

Her mom patted her arm before moving on to speak with a trio of couples congregating near where Pops was holding court. Cec checked the kitchen table where she had laid out a buffet of finger foods and watched as guests filled their plates, and headed out through the open patio doors to the backyard.

Cec also checked to make sure all the

drinks were filled, then changed direction and ran into a wall of muscle. It was her brother. "BJ, Mom's been looking for you."

"I just found her a second ago." He rubbed his jaw, his expression neutral. "Pops looks pretty good tonight."

"Yeah, pretty good given what he's going through."

BJ paused, dropping his voice as he said, "I can't believe these few days will probably be the last time that I have with him. I mean, we've been talking on the phone, but it's not the same as in person. Thank you for pushing me to come and visit."

"Thank you for showing up. It's meant a lot to him." She gave him a big, warm smile. "And to me too. And Mom."

He smiled back, took a deep breath and grabbed one of the plastic cups with lemonade. "I'll catch up with you later, yeah?"

She noticed he went straight for Pops. Her brother being the joker he was, he then veered off without a word before turning around and laughing with Pops. Pops got to his feet and embraced her brother, then sat back down, BJ taking a seat on the grass at his feet.

"Who's that big guy talking to Burt? He looks familiar."

Cec turned to find Gus watching the proceedings. "When did you get here?"

He smiled. "Just now. Thought I'd start with what's happening in the kitchen. The best parties always happen in the kitchen." He leaned forward as if to get a better view of BJ. "Is that your brother?"

She nodded and smiled as she heard Pops laughing heartily at something her brother said. "That's him."

"I don't know what I expected, but he doesn't look like you at all."

"I take after my dad's side while BJ is all my mom."

Gus's mom walked up to her and gave her a quick hug. "Thank you again for the invite to the party tonight. Is there anything I can do to help?"

Cec shook her head. "I think everything is all set for now. And you're our guest. Please go and enjoy yourself."

His mom gave Gus a smile, then started to fill a plate with food before grabbing a drink and heading outside. Cec turned to Gus. "How was your trip? We haven't really gotten a chance to speak since you've been back."

She wondered at the flash of something sad in his eyes. But then he suddenly grinned as if she hadn't seen anything. "Good. It's so beautiful up there. And I have a lot to talk to you about."

"So, you did take the job?"

Her mom entered the kitchen and held up her phone. "She just pulled up out front."

Cec apologized to Gus and pointed to the living room. "Sorry, I've got to go take care of this."

Out front, Phyllis and her granddaughter exited a car and walked up the sidewalk to the porch. Cec took the few steps down to greet the older woman. "Thank you for coming. When I called with the invitation, I wasn't sure if you would agree."

"You were right. This is a much better way to say goodbye." She glanced over Cec's shoulder. "And he doesn't know that I'm coming?"

"We wanted to surprise him."

"And not disappoint him if I didn't show, right?" The older woman smiled. "It's okay, dear. You only want to protect Burt."

They walked along the pathway to the backyard, and Cec knew the moment that Pops realized Phyllis was there. He stopped talking mid-sentence, stared at Phyllis, then opened his arms. She rushed into them and embraced him. "I'm sorry, I'm sorry."

"I was the one who told you to leave."

"But I could have insisted on staying."

Pops held her hand and gestured to BJ with the other. "This is my grandson that I was telling you about. BJ, this is Phyllis."

BJ shook her hand. "He's told me all about you these last couple of days."

Phyllis turned to Pops. "You have?"

Pops colored.

"Phyllis is here." Gus's tone was full of affection.

Cec noted him standing beside her. She gave a nod. "I invited her."

He looked at her, smiling. "That was a good call. And Burt seems to agree." He reached out and took her hand. "There's something I'd like to—"

"Hey, everyone. Pops wants to say something," BJ announced to the large gang of well-wishers.

People left the kitchen and walked out

to join the rest of the guests. Pops stood as people surrounded him and he held on to BJ's arm on one side and Phyllis's on the other. "First, I appreciate you coming tonight. I know it's not usual to have a going-away party like this, so thank you for indulging an old man's whims. You have all been important to me. Loved and cherished. And I hope to spend time with each one of you tonight to say goodbye." He glanced at Phyllis who blushed.

"But before that, I'd like to share something important. As I near the end of my life, the only things I regret are the things I didn't do. Even the mistakes I made, they contributed to who I am." He paused and tightened his grip on BJ's arm. "I'm not perfect and am sure no saint, but I've tried my best and it's been an amazing life. So happy with the people I've been fortunate to meet, to spend time with, to love.

"You know, there comes a time when it's not the possessions you have or the house you own. It's not the clothes in your closet or the number attached to your savings account. When you get down to it, what really matters is what you share with others and what they're willing to share with you. That's the real gift."

Pops turned, and Cec could swear he was looking right at her. "So if there's something I could leave you with tonight, it's this. Always take a chance to find happiness. And if you fall, get up and try again. And again, and again."

He sat down, and everyone clapped, as several people came forward to talk to him. Gus turned to Cec. "Do you think we could find a quiet place to talk?"

Why did that sound ominous? Was he going to tell her he took the job? She scanned the bustling yard, then pointed to the house. "It might be quieter inside."

He agreed and followed her via the kitchen into the living room. She wasn't sure she wanted answers or not, but she faced him. "You're taking the job, aren't you?"

He shook his head. "No."

"But it's perfect for you. You'll get your adventures while using your medical training. Why would you turn that down?"

"It doesn't have everything I want."

"What else could you possibly want?"

He took a step forward and put his hands on her hips. "You." He looked at her as if he could see all the way through to her soul. She liked that feeling. Warm and safe. "I was going to take the job when I left here, but I couldn't get you out of my head. And then my mom showed up. And between what she told me and what Burt said tonight, it only tells me I'm making the right decision and…

"I thought I couldn't go the distance not just with you, but with anyone. Two-time loser in the marriage department doesn't add up to a secure future."

"And now?"

"Now…" He put a finger under her chin and lifted her head so that he could look directly into her eyes. "My past doesn't dictate my future. I can be a forever kind of man because of you—you're my forever."

She shook her head. "None of this changes the fact that we're too different."

"But different in a good way."

"What? Like in opposites attract?"

"I wouldn't reduce what we have to a cliché."

"But we don't have anything, Gus. We

had a few kisses and some long talks, but it takes a lot more than that to make a relationship."

"I don't know what the future holds, Cec. But what I do know is that I want you to be a part of it. The question is, do you want me to be a part of yours?"

Someone cleared their throat behind them, and Cec turned to find one of Pops's old friends standing there. "Cecily, I'm sorry to interrupt, but can you tell me where the bathroom is?"

GUS WAITED ON the edge of the crowd that had lined up to get a moment with Burt. The old man looked worn out from the evening's festivities, but Gus knew he would spend time with each person before he'd call it a night no matter how tired he got.

When Gus walked up to him, Burt held up a finger. "I need to talk to you about something, but I want to wait until this crowd leaves. Would you mind staying to help me to bed after the party?"

"Of course."

Which is why he found himself picking up empty cups and plates and stuffing them into a garbage bag as the last few stragglers said their goodbyes to Burt. When the remaining guests finally left the backyard, Burt sat down again, his shoulders slumped. Gus rushed to his side. "You doing okay?"

"Just tired." He glanced around the backyard. "Did you see where they put my walker? It was getting in the way, so I had BJ put it aside. Maybe the kitchen?"

"I'll get it." Gus walked that way and stopped short when he found Cec standing at the kitchen sink, the water running, her head down, her shoulders shaking. He came alongside her. "What's wrong, Cec?"

She turned away and wiped her face. "Nothing. I'm just done in from all the planning for the party."

"You should be proud. You did a good job tonight. I know Burt is happy, and a lot of guests were commenting on how nice everything was." She gave a nod and went back to rinsing dishes and placing them in the dishwasher. He asked, "Have you seen Burt's walker? He thinks BJ brought it inside and left it somewhere."

She glanced over her shoulder. "I think I saw it in the living room."

Gus patted her on the back, letting his hand rest there for a moment. "It's okay to cry. You've been doing a lot of work these past couple of weeks. But I'm back now. I can give you a hand with everything around here."

"And my mom is moving in next week to help too."

"Good." He let his hand drop. "Well, I'll help Burt get ready for bed."

"Your mom asked me to tell you that she went back to your house."

"Thank you."

He found the walker and took it outside with him. Burt grunted as he stood up from the lawn chair and steadied himself on the walker before making the journey inside. Gus followed behind in case he was needed.

After Burt had finished in the bathroom, Gus helped the older man get changed out of his party clothes and into pajamas. When Burt fumbled with the buttons, Gus took over and finished fastening the top. "Stupid fingers are useless these days."

"It's okay. I've got this."

Once in his pajamas, Gus helped him to

the bed and checked the oxygen level on the condenser. Burt sat on the edge of the bed and took a deep breath, adjusting the cannula in his nose. "This dying business is getting old. I'm worn out from it."

"I know."

Burt looked up at him. "I worry about Cecily. She's going to take my passing really hard."

"I'll be here to help her. I promise." He peered at the older man. "Is that what you wanted to talk to me about?"

"No, but it's related." He inhaled and exhaled another deep breath. "Only a fool would let a woman like Cecily get away from him."

"Maybe she's the one who doesn't want to be with me." After all, she hadn't answered his question about making a future together.

"Then you haven't said the right words to convince her."

He thought about the conversation they'd started earlier. He'd asked her if she wanted to be in his life, thought he'd made a persuasive case for them, but then they'd been interrupted. And the moment had passed without her really stating her side of things. Gus sighed and took a seat next to Burt on the bed. "It's not that simple."

"Sure, it is. Do you love her?"

He turned to look at Burt. "I really do."

"And do you think she loves you?"

He gave a shrug. "I think she does."

"Have you asked her?"

"I tried. Do you think she does?"

The old man nodded. "You love her. She loves you. It's simple."

"No offense, Burt, but nothing's ever that simple."

"I never expected to see Phyllis again, but when she stepped into the backyard tonight, it was like my heart had found its beat. It was that easy. And I think your heart has found its beat with Cecily. So when we're finished here, you go into the kitchen and tell her you love her and ask her if she loves you. Start from there."

"And if she says she doesn't?"

"I'm sure she'll give you a bunch of reasons it won't work out with you two, but you tell her all the reasons it will."

He sighed again. "We've both been burned

before with our past marriages, which makes us cautious."

"Since when has being in love ever been about caution? It's the riskiest thing in the world." Burt's eyes were still on him. "But let me tell you, it's the only thing worth living for. It's like I said earlier. It's the only thing that matters in the end."

Gus nodded. "You're right. I'll talk to her."

"Good." Gus stood and helped Burt swing his legs into bed. "I need to know I'm leaving her in capable hands. After all I did on our trip to get the two of you together, it would be a shame to see all that hard work go to waste."

Gus snapped his fingers. "I knew you were up to something. Not that you were trying to be very subtle."

Pops chuckled. "You're a good man, Gus. I know you'll make her happy."

He could only hope that he would. Gus walked to the door and turned out the light. "Good night, Burt."

"Good night, son."

THE DISHWASHER FULL and running, Cec wiped down the kitchen counters with a rag. She looked up when Gus entered the room. "Thank you for getting Pops into bed."

He smiled, and she returned to cleaning, but Gus approached her and put his hand on hers. "I know you want to clean up after the party, but do you mind if we talk for a moment?"

"Gus, it's been a long day. I'm tired. And I just want to finish this and go to bed."

"I'll help you finish and then we can talk."

"Fine."

As she wiped the counters and the kitchen table, Gus checked the backyard and turned off lights and shut and locked the doors. Within moments, they were finished and sitting on the sofa in the living room. She looked at him. "So, talk."

Gus reached for her. "I love you, Cec. With all my heart. And I want to know if you love me too."

She tried to understand what he said. "You love me?"

He nodded and squeezed her hand. "That's what I've been trying to tell you before, but it's always one thing or another keeping us apart." He looked so handsome, so genuine. Was this her chance finally at that kind of love she'd been hoping for? "But you didn't answer the question, Cec. Do you love me?"

Of course she did. But eventually he was going to leave, and she was going to stay and it didn't change the fact that they were wrong for each other. "What does it matter? It would never work between us."

"I've been thinking about what you said. That we're opposites. And you're right. We are. You are overly cautious, and I take risks. You like your schedules and routines while I crave spontaneity. I don't see those parts of us changing anytime soon, do you?"

If he was trying to convince her to be with him, he wasn't starting out very well. She narrowed her eyes at him. "Where are you going with this?"

"That our differences complement, not contradict each other. I'm a risk-taker, but I need you to keep me grounded. I fly by the seat of my pants most of the time, but I need you to steady our ship. You're my gravity."

That didn't sound like it was a good thing, but it reminded her of what Pops had said. That she could be his anchor and that was a great thing. "And gravity? That's what you want?"

"No, it's what I need. You're amazing and special and the only one for me, Cec."

"Sounds like you've figured it all out. But what do I need?"

"You need me to shake you up sometimes and get you out of your comfort zone. You need the fire of my passion to balance out your cool logic. I'm your wings to help you fly."

He reached up with his free hand and stroked her cheek. "So long as we love each other, we'll make it work. Your grandfather's right. Love *is* simple. We're the ones making it hard."

He smiled at her and she felt the warmth down to her toes. "So let me ask you again, do you love me?"

She looked into his eyes and saw the sincerity there. He did love her and meant every word he'd said. Fear wanted to keep her feelings, her words inside, but love won out. "I do."

Gus pulled her in close for a kiss, which she returned with relish. This felt right, she knew it now and leaned into it with every feeling and instinct she had.

The kiss ended and she opened her eyes to stare into his. "I love you, Gus."

"For as long as I have a heartbeat, I love you too."

EPILOGUE

CEC STOOD AT the edge of the waterfall, holding Gus's hand. "I don't know about this. I still haven't gotten over the trau— oh, er, the excitement of skydiving."

"What are you talking about? You did great."

"Only because I had you right there."

"And you have me right here too. For better or worse. Isn't that what we promised?"

Cec turned and smiled at her husband of six days. "We did. But I don't think I promised to jump off cliffs with you."

"This isn't a cliff. It's only about twelve feet up from the surface of the lake. Besides, it's smaller than the one I tried to get you to jump off last summer. It's perfectly safe."

"I know. I did the research and checked. There's never been a casualty reported here."

"Then what are we waiting for?" He tugged her closer. "Burt would want us to enjoy this time together. And to take a chance or two."

"I can't believe it's been almost a year since he's been gone." She swallowed at the familiar ache in her chest when she remembered Pops. He'd finally succumbed to the cancer a couple weeks after his going-away party, surrounded by her mom, Gus and herself. She blinked away the mist in her eyes. "And he would want me to take a chance on this jump. Just like I took a chance on you."

Gus gave her a quick, sweet kiss, then inched forward. She followed. "Ready? We'll jump together on three."

"And you won't let go of my hand?"

"Never." He grinned at her, then squeezed her hand and walked her closer to the edge. "Okay. One. Two… Three!"

They jumped as one, and a few seconds later plunged into the lake, their hands still entwined. When they surfaced for air, Gus pulled her against his chest, so close she could feel his heart beating as fast as hers.

She let out a whoop of victory and couldn't wait to jump again.

* * * * *